Souvenir

A Tom Donovan Mystery

David Coleman

NFB
<<<>>>
Buffalo, NY

No Frills Buffalo/Amelia Press
119 Dorchester Road
Buffalo, New York 14213

For more information please visit

Nofrillsbuffalo.com

In Loving Memory

Loretta Coleman

1923-2015

A Life Lived with Grace

More Tom Donovan Mysteries

Available Now

Rust Belt Redemption

Two years ago Tom Donovan was a cop, working the rough and tumble streets of Buffalo's East side. One fateful night he was involved in the deaths of a Federal agent and an unarmed man. Fast forward to the present; Donovan is now working as an operative for a private investigator. His latest assignment is to locate the wife of Gary Shields, a local real estate mogul. His investigation leads him to a seamy underside of Shields' business interests and he is forced to make a choice between doing his job and answering to his conscience.

Shadow Boxing

Buffalo New York Ex cop Tom Donovan is struggling with the events of his recent past, both physically and mentally, when an event from twenty two years ago captures his attention. Hank "Lights Out" Loughran, Tom's trainer when he was an aspiring boxer, tells Tom that his father's death, declared an accident over twenty years ago, wasn't all that it appeared to be. Tom sets off on a private mission to uncover the truth.

Souvenir

A Tom Donavan Mystery

Prologue I

September 1993

The first day of school was over. The boy got off the bus on the corner of Seneca Street and Unger Avenue. He had told his mom that he was old enough to walk home from the bus stop by himself, hoping that she wouldn't embarrass him in front of his new schoolmates. He was relieved to see that she wasn't there.

A few other kids had gotten off at the stop. None of them appeared to be that friendly with one another so in a way it was a relief to the boy that he wouldn't be a total outsider, destined to be on the outs with any established clique. He had had enough of that at his old school in Riverside. He had always been quiet and had tried to blend in. The trouble started when the big mouth, Jerry Rydzinski, had found out his mother worked at the Colonial Lounge and started telling everyone that the boy's mom was a stripper. The boy had told them that his mother was a bartender but Rydzinski had only laughed and told him that his older brother had been to the Colonial and seen his mother taking her clothes off and hustling tips from perverts. The boy wanted to punch Rydzinski right in his lying mouth, but Rydzinski was bigger and his friends were hanging around to see if he could get a rise out of him.

The only thing that the boy knew about his real father was that he had been a minor league baseball player. He had a one-year contract with the Indians and had spent one summer with the Bisons. He met his mother while she was working at a bar near the stadium and they dated and moved in together. Then, the baseball player was waived by the Indians and with no prospects he moved back to his native Florida, leaving behind a cracked bat and a pregnant girlfriend.

One day his mom had told him they were moving in with Donny. Donny worked as a mechanic at a gas station and she found a place in South Buffalo on Unger. It was going to be different. It had only been him and his mom as long as he could remember and he liked it that way. There was a parade of baby sitters when his mom worked her shift at the bar and most of them were nice, and his mother always seemed to be able to weed out the bad ones. She told him she was tired though and needed to settle into some kind of normal life. She wanted to get a day job where she wouldn't have to be out all night and she could spend more time with him.

Right after they moved in with Donny the situation became stressful. During the brief period that Donny and his mother had dated, Donny seemed to take little interest in the boy. His mother had told him to give it time, Donny hadn't been around kids all that much. After they moved in Donny became at first irritable and then downright hostile. The kid couldn't seem to do anything right and was always making a mess. Donny and his mom used to argue about Donny and his friends making too much noise and smoking pot late at night when the kid was in bed.

As the summer wore on the arguments got worse and covered a wider range of topics. Then one morning after the boy had heard the adults arguing the night before, he saw the bruises on her arm. Even at eleven years of age he recognized the marks left by a man's grip. Another time there was a welt on his mother's cheek. When he asked her about it she just said she had bumped into a post in the basement when she was getting the laundry.

It came to a head the week before school started. Donny had apparently lost his job at the garage and told the boy's mom he could make more money selling weed anyway. She'd had enough though. She told him that it was her name on the lease and she wasn't going to share her apartment with a drug dealer.

The boy remembered being in his room and listening to them argue. He had only been to church a few times in his life, before his grandparents passed, but that night he prayed. He prayed for the argument to stop and for Donny to just go ahead and leave. He was saying a Hail Mary when he heard a crash. He went to his closet, grabbed his father's bat, and rushed out of his room, terrified of what he might find.

Donny was gone. His mother was standing in the living room, looking over the broken remains of the coffee table, holding her lower back and wincing. She looked up saw the boy, then wiped her eyes and told him that it was just going to be the two of them again, at least for a while.

As he walked down the block, a cloud swept across the sky, temporarily blocking the sun. The air held its first hint of autumn. The cloud moved on and the sun came out again, warming his face. Maybe now they could be happy.

He climbed the porch steps and went to the door on the right, the one that led to the upper flat.

The door was open, his mother probably had come home with an armload of groceries and forgot to close it. It was Tuesday, her night off. That meant she would be making a good dinner and there wouldn't be a sitter.

He went up the stairs to the door to the flat; it was also ajar. As he looked at it more closely he saw that the wood on the doorjamb was splintered where the faceplate had been. His heart sank. Immediately he thought the worst. It had been too easy, too perfect a solution. He walked into the apartment and thought about calling out to his mother, but the silence was pressing down on him and he couldn't find the breath.

He found her in the kitchen lying in front of the stove. There was a pool of blood under her head and her eyes were open. Her skin was white and her face seemed frozen in a surprised expression. Even though he was only a child himself, he knew his mother was dead.

Prologue II

March, 1967

Hugh Donovan sat at the bar, counting the day's receipts. It had been a slow night. The weather outside was horrendous. It had been raining and sleeting all day. Tomorrow would be better though. Starting at 8 AM the third shift workers from Republic Steel would roll in, paychecks in hand, ready to be cashed (minus a five percent fee of course.) Tabs would be paid and bets would be placed and the wheel would turn again.

He looked up as the door opened and the young man walked in. Marty, the thick necked bartender with the crooked nose also looked up from where he was washing glasses and said, "We're closed kid. Beat it."

The young man just stood there. Hugh noticed that he was soaked to the skin. His windbreaker was shiny with precipitation and his denim work shirt was an unnaturally dark blue. He was rail thin but had broad shoulders and large hands.

"Are you deaf?" Marty asked gruffly. "I said we're closed."

The kid cleared his throat and looked at Marty. "I was hoping to speak to Morris Donovan," he said.

Marty looked puzzled and looked to Hugh for guidance. Hugh shook his head at Marty and then the bar man took his hand off the sawed off baseball bat that was hung under the bar.

"What would you be wanting with my father?" Hugh asked, placing his cigarette in the ashtray on the bar.

The young man looked at Hugh as if trying to size him up. Then he spoke, "I was hoping to talk to him about a job."

Hugh sat back in the vinyl-covered barstool and picked up the cigarette. "Well, there's two problems then: first, my father passed away four years ago. Second, we ain't hiring."

The young man looked crestfallen. His eyes fell to the mud caked boots on his feet and he just stood there. He looked up slowly and said, "I'm sorry for your loss."

Hugh took a drag and looked at the back of the bar through the smoke he exhaled. "Not as sorry as he is." He looked at the young man more intently. "Tell me something lad," he said. "If you know my dad well enough to ask for him, how did you not know he was dead?"

"I've been away," the young man said looking up again.

"Fair enough. So why would my dad, or I for that matter, take on such a sorry individual as yourself."

The kid, instead of shrinking at the dig, seemed to take on a little resolve. "My pop used to work for your dad. He brought me here a few times when I was barely old enough to remember."

"And who would your dad be?" Hugh asked.

"Stanley Czerny."

Hugh thought for a moment. Then a light seemed to come on. "Polack Stan? He's been dead for what?"

"Twelve years."

Marty looked even more confused. Hugh noticed this and said, "It's okay Marty. You can go home. Just do me a favor and set us up with a bottle and two glasses. And none of that cheap shit we give to the masses." He looked over at the kid and said, "Have a seat son." Then he pulled out the stool next to his.

Marty got a bottle of Seagram's V.O. off the back bar and produced two tumblers from a shelf. As he set them in front of Hugh he raised his eyebrows.

"Go home Marty. I want to hear what young Mr. Czerny has to say for himself."

Marty shot the young man one more dirty look, left the bar and went into a back room.

"I said have a seat son. Let's call this a job interview."

The young man peeled off the windbreaker and hung it on a coat rack by the door. Hugh thought he should be shivering, he looked so wet and cold. His skin was as pale as could be and his close-cropped blond hair was reflecting the light from behind the bar. The kid was holding it together though. He had self-assurance without the cockiness that Hugh found so irritating with a lot of the local punks. He sat down on the stool next to Hugh's.

Hugh reached for the bottle and poured three fingers worth into his glass and then pointed the bottle at the kid's as he looked at him.

"No thank you, Mr. Donovan," the young man said. "I don't drink the hard stuff."

'Hmm," Hugh said. "Well, that's one thing that you don't have in common with your old man."

The kid was either too dim to recognize another dig or didn't let on that it bothered him. He looked straight at Hugh and said, "They told my Ma he was drunk when he fell into the machinery at the grain mill, so I suppose you're right."

"What's your name son?"

"Francis, sir."

"How old are you, Francis?"

"Eighteen."

Hugh smiled wryly and took a drink. "If you lie to me again I'll toss you back out in the rain, Francis."

For the first time the kid was taken aback. He composed himself quickly and said, "I'm sixteen. I'll be seventeen in two months."

Hugh lit another cigarette and sat back. "Do you know what your dad did for my dad?"

"No, sir. Like I said I can barely remember coming here. I know he used to bring paper bags in every Friday. My dad would bring me in sometimes if my mom was ill and let me play shuffle board."

Hugh seemed to be lost in a memory. He flicked his ash and said, "It was union business, that's all." He shook his head. "I knew your pop, he was a good guy. My dad liked him too, he was dependable to a fault unless he had a snoot full." Hugh glanced at Francis. "How old were you when?"

"I was six."

"That's rough. How'd your mom take it?"

Francis smiled, as if remembering something. "Not well. My mother was never the picture of health and after dad's accident she couldn't take care of me or my sister. I think she wound up at the psych center on Elmwood."

Hugh narrowed his eyes at Francis. "So where did you wind up then?"

"Father Baker's."

"No shit?"

"No sir. My baby sister got adopted right away and I never heard of her again. I was there 'til they closed the orphanage in '56 and then I went to a foster home."

"Someplace nice?"

Francis grimaced. "Not exactly..."

Hugh turned his palms up to try to get Francis to continue.

Francis' cheeks colored ever so slightly. "It's just that..." he paused.

"What is it son? Out with it."

"It's just that this is the part of the story that may cause you to question my character."

Hugh laughed. "Hell son, if there is one thing this place has it's an abundance of characters."

"I lived with the Swaiteks in Kaisertown for three and a half years and you could say I left under a cloud," Francis said looking up at Hugh again.

"Go on."

"You gotta understand Mr. Donovan. Swaitek was only in it for the money the state sent his way to take us in. There were four of us in a dirty, windowless room. And the old man was quick with a belt when he was angry, which was quite often. One night, shortly after I turned twelve he was about to give me a whipping when I had enough and pushed his fat ass down the stairs." Francis stopped and glanced at Hugh to see how that admission had gone over.

"Hmm, and did that earn you a few extra lashes?"

"No, sir. Swaitek broke his neck in the fall and we were all removed from the home."

"So, some good came of it then."

Francis shook his head. "To a point, sir. I was sent to the Stafford Home for Boys outside of Utica."

Hugh lit another cigarette and poured himself another whiskey. "I know a few Stafford alumni. They don't have very fond memories of the place."

"Nor should they. Most of the boys who get out wind up in Attica eventually."

"So when were you let out?"

Francis hesitated for a moment and then went on, "I wasn't let out, sir. I left."

Hugh sat up. "You ran away?"

"You could say that, sir. There was a spot of trouble and I lit out."

"How much trouble are we talking about?"

"A lot of trouble." Suddenly the words were coming out faster, as if Francis was at confession and he wanted to unburden himself. "There was a fight at mess one night and me and my friend Eddie were unjustly accused of starting it. I swear Mr. Donovan, we were only defending ourselves. But the Bulls saw it otherwise and we were cut down to half rations and given extra work in the field. Well, Eddie stole some food from the kitchen and we thought we got away with it, until we got ratted out by a snitch on our ward. A few days later we got a hold of the snitch on a work detail and dragged him into the woods. Eddie was giving him a good going over when one of Bulls comes up on us and whacks Eddie over the head."

"And you jumped the guard?" Hugh asked.

Francis gritted his teeth and went on, "Well sir, ordinarily I wouldn't even consider such a thing but it was Burke, the worst of the bulls. That same night stick he was hitting Lenny with... what he used to do with that..."

Hugh squinted at Francis but said nothing.

Francis was fighting it but his eyes were starting to fill. "If he caught up to you in the shower he would..."

"I get the picture," Hugh said.

"Well before I knew what I was doing, I took my spade and whacked Burke over the head with it. I just wanted to stop him but his skull cracked open and he dropped like a sack of potatoes."

"Jesus," was all Hugh could manage.

"Yes sir, I know. If I had to do it all over again I wouldn't." Francis blinked and looked down at the bar.

"What did you do then?" Hugh asked.

"Well, Eddie is in a panic. He grabs the snitch and says we have to do him too. We can't leave no witnesses. I was just standing there with the shovel in my hand looking down at Burke. The snitch is swearing on his mother's soul that he won't tell no one. All I can think is I'll be tried as an adult and get the chair. I tell the kid to clear out and as he turns around I whack him too. Only he doesn't die right away. He's just lying there and moaning. I tried to give the shovel to Eddie to finish him but he pushes it back at me and says he can't. After listening to the poor bastard moaning in the dirt for what seemed like forever I finally dropped down to my knees and choked him out of his misery. It was getting near dark so we dragged them to a marshy spot in the woods and buried them. I told Lenny we should head for the fence but all of a sudden he starts going on about how I did Burke and the snitch and he shouldn't have to pay for what I did. I just looked at him and then I chucked the shovel and headed for the fence.

Hugh looked thoughtfully at his glass. "And this Eddie, he stayed behind?"

"I don't know, sir. I hightailed it out of there and didn't look back."

"When was this?"

Francis exhaled, seemingly relieved that his story was out. "Ten days ago, I hitched my way back here."

"What did you do for food?"

"I'm afraid I pilfered from a few farms and a supermarket in Henrietta."

"I see," Hugh said smiling slightly.

"I'm not a thief sir. It's just that–"

"Take it easy kid," Hugh said and raised a hand cutting him off. He finished his whiskey and stubbed out his cigarette. "I'll tell you what. I'm going to go against my better judgment and take you on."

Francis brightened and said, "Mr. Donovan. I can't tell you-"

"It's strictly probationary," Hugh cut him off. "On one hand, I like a guy who sticks up for himself and his friends and thinks on his feet."

"Thank you, Mr. Don-"

Hugh's hand came up again. "On the other hand, I don't need some clown working for me who is going to lose his head every time he's under the gun. There's a time to fight and a time to negotiate."

Francis just looked at him and Hugh went on, "Do you understand?"

"I think so sir."

"Good. Now you and I are going to go into the back and make a couple of sandwiches. After that you can use one of the cots upstairs and maybe take a shower." Hugh looked him up and down. "I got a kid about your size. I'll see if he has some old clothes for you until you get on your feet."

"Thank you, Mr. Donovan."

Hugh paused for a second and put an index finger to his lip. "I think we better give you an alias while you're here."

"If you say so, sir."

Hugh smiled and turned towards the kitchen. "Well, first of all, I don't think we can have a Polack working at Donovan's, so from now on we'll call you by the name of an old friend of mine from the First Ward."

Francis knew better than to argue. "What name would that be?"

"His last name was Brennan. First was Roger." Hugh turned at the door before going in. "You don't look like a Roger though."

Francis shrugged. "How about Francis then?"

"No, Francis sounds kinda queer. No offense..."

"None taken. How about Frank?"

Hugh shook his head. "I already got two Franks on the payroll and four or five more who are regulars. I'm up to my ass in Franks." Then he looked hard at Francis. "But I'll be damned if you're not the whitest Polack I have ever seen. From now on you'll be known as Whitey Brennan."

Chapter 1

From The Buffalo News, June 14, 2014.

Hugh L. Donovan - Local businessman, tavern owner.

Hugh L. Donovan, long time owner of a South Buffalo family business, passed away on Friday June 13 after a long illness. Mr. Donovan inherited the business from his father Morris Donovan in 1964 and ran it until his passing. He also had numerous real estate holdings throughout the Buffalo area. He is preceded in death by his wife Maureen (Murphy), his brother Clancy and son Thomas Sr. (Rosalie). He is survived by his grandson Thomas Jr. Visitation will be held at the O'Connell-Murphy Funeral home on South Park Ave. Monday from 10:00 AM to 1:00 PM and from 7:00 PM to 9:00 PM. A mass of Christian burial will take place on Tuesday at 10:00 AM at Holy Family CC.

The obituary didn't even scratch the surface as far as Tom Donovan was concerned. His grandfather had been much more than a simple tavern owner and "businessman." During Hugh Donovan's long life, he had taken his own father's business, started with the seeds of bootlegging money from the thirties, and grown it into a small fiefdom. In its heyday the Tavern was like a lot of other bars that popped up around the steel plants and the docks. Hugh was visionary enough to know that things ran in cycles and he needed to diversify. So there was bookmaking, loan sharking and a smattering of "union business" that kept the family business profitable long after the manufacturing might of the city began to ebb.

Tom had to wonder what it all meant in the end. Hugh had lost a lot over the years, his wife, his brother, a granddaughter and his only son. The only thing he had left, as far as Tom knew was the bar and a grandson who had preferred to keep his distance from the family business. The ultimate slap in the face came when Tom, at the urging of his maternal uncle, went the other way and became a cop. Things had been reserved at the best of times, and downright hostile at the worst. None of that changed much when Tom lost his badge after a shooting at the McKinley Projects. Hugh had expected that Tom might come around but that never transpired. They had one last run in over a year ago, when Hugh took his vengeance on the two men responsible for the deaths of his son and granddaughter. Tom had witnessed the execution and while he had briefly considered turning the old man in, he realized that he had the same hunger for payback that Hugh had exercised. Besides, Hugh was dying. His doctors had told him he had less than a year.

Tom had attended both parts of the wake, as much as he could stand. A crowd of older people had shuffled into the Funeral Home to pay their respects. He was surprised when several of his colleagues from the former Frederickson and Associates detective agency showed up. Sherry Palkowski, now Buffalo PD herself, came during the morning visitation. She stayed for a while and excused herself when she had to report for duty downtown. Grace Frederickson also stopped by. Tom hadn't seen Grace since she dissolved the agency after the death of her husband Cal. Tom was glad to see Grace but his stomach still tied itself in a knot, knowing that Cal was killed by a man who was actually trying to kill Tom. Cal was one of the ghosts who still appeared to Tom in his dreams. He had thought that with the passage of time some of the memories would be easier, but they weren't. If anything, there were just more of them.

His mother had surprised him when she said she wanted to attend the funeral the next day. Hugh was, after all, she explained, still her father-in-law. Tom picked her up at 9:00. She was dressed in a simple dark gray dress and Tom noticed that she looked different. Her hair, still dark with a few streaks of silver, appeared to have been cut and styled. For years she had just worn it straight or pulled back with very little flare. There was something else that he noticed. Still pretty at sixty-three, his mother had always had an air of melancholy about her, especially since the death of her daughter and then the death of Tom's father. Today though, there seemed to be a lightness about her. She was still not what you would call loquacious, especially considering the occasion, but she seemed different. Tom made a mental note to ask her about it at a more appropriate time.

The funeral was a somber affair. A lot of old timers from the neighborhood and a few people Tom didn't recognize. To his chagrin, he was asked to be a pallbearer. It was Tom, Whitey Brennan, Whitey's two sons and two of the regulars from the tavern who looked old enough to be inside the box instead of carrying it. After the mass, Hugh's remains were taken to the cemetery in the warm spring sunshine.

Then Hugh was laid to rest between his wife and his son.

Tom was walking back to his car with his mother when a voice called out to him, "Tommy!" He turned around to see Whitey walking towards them putting a handkerchief back in his pocket.

Whitey looked past Tom and said, "Rose, it's good to see you. Sorry it had to be under these circumstances."

To Tom's surprise Rose walked up to Whitey and gave him a peck on the cheek. "Good to see you too, Francis. How is Connie?"

"She's fine. As a matter of fact, we're all headed over to the bar to have a more traditional Irish wake, if you'd care to join us."
Rose smiled and said, "I would love to, but I have an appointment I just can't miss."

Whitey nodded and said, "Of course. Some other time. We'd love to have you and Tom over for dinner some night."

"Well that sounds lovely. As soon as Tom drops me off I'll make sure he comes right back."

Tom started to cringe but caught himself and put on a smile for Whitey. He really didn't feel like standing around listening to people with selective memory go on about what a great guy Hugh Donovan had been while they tied one on.

Whitey looked back at him and asked, "What do you say Tom? I'd like to talk to you about a few things as well, if you have the time."

"Of course. I'll be there in about an hour," Tom said, offering his hand to Whitey.

Rose Donovan had been living with her brother Samuel since an acquaintance of Tom's had threatened her the year before. The threat had passed, but her brother had already put the house she had been living in up for sale. Tom and his mother had been quiet on the first part of the ride to North Buffalo but then his curiosity got the better of him.

"So, Mom, do you really have an appointment or did you just want to avoid going to the Tavern?" He smiled as he said it to let her know it wasn't an accusation.

His mother was half turned towards the passenger side window and he saw the corner of her mouth turn up. She turned to him and said, "You know how I feel about that place, Tom. But to answer your question, yes I, do have an engagement."

"An engagement?"

She looked straight ahead through the windshield and stated, "Well if you must know, Mr. Nosey Detective, I have a date."

Tom's head shot around to look at his mother with his mouth open. Out of the corner of his eye he saw a pair of brake lights come on and barely stopped before rear-ending the car in front of him.

After a moment's silence Rose looked at her son and the frightened look she had turned to a smile, "Mary Mother of God, Tom. We've already had one funeral today."

The light turned green and Tom eased up on the death grip he had on the steering wheel and gently accelerated. "A date?" was all he could manage.

"I know it sounds crazy, right?"

"No, Ma. It's just that I didn't know you were seeing someone."

They pulled down his uncle's street and Rose looked at Tom again. "His name is Anthony and I met him at church. Actually I shouldn't say met him. I knew him from the neighborhood. We bumped into each other at the church bazaar and started talking. Next thing you know he asked me out and I said what the hell, why not."

Tom's head was spinning. This was uncharted territory. "How long?"

"Just a couple of months." They pulled into his uncle's driveway and Tom put the car in park.

Rose put a hand on his cheek. "Don't look so serious Tom. It's just been a couple of dates."

"I know but..."

"But what?"

Tom shook his head. "Who is this guy?"

Rose laughed, a sound Tom hadn't heard in a long time. "Are you worried that you won't approve?"

Tom couldn't help but smile to see his mother actually enjoying something, even if it was her teasing him. "Well I think I should meet this man before I give him my blessing."

"You little snot," Rose started. She stopped and squinted. "You know what? That's a great idea. Let's have dinner."

Tom's smile slipped away. "What?"

"I think you'll like him Tom and I've told him about you. How about this Friday?"

"I'm... okay... where?"

"Lombardo's, say seven o'clock?"

"Yeah, I can do that." The words left Tom's mouth seemingly without him willing them to.

Rose leaned over and kissed him on the cheek. "Thank you, love," she said. "Maybe after you meet him and give him your blessing, you could talk to Sam."

Tom was confused. "Talk to Sam about what?"

"Well, he doesn't know that I'm seeing Anthony. We may need to soften him up a bit." She started to climb out of the car.

"Mom, why would we need to soften Uncle Sam up?"

She looked back in. "Oh, when Anthony was younger he got into a little bit of trouble."

"How much is a little bit?"

"Well..." she appeared to be choosing her words carefully. "He was in jail for a little while."

Tom was struck speechless again. His mind was racing so fast that he had no reply when his mother said, "Thank you Tom. We'll see you Friday. I love you." With that she shut the door and walked lightly up the driveway to the side door.

Tom finally got his mouth to move.

"Shit."

Chapter 2

Donovan's head was still reeling from the conversation he'd had with his mother earlier. He found a parking spot several blocks away from the tavern on South Park Ave. He was sure that the extra cars near the bar could only mean that the place was full of mourners, friends or other people looking for free booze. It had warmed up considerably so he left his jacket and tie in the Chevy and made his way back up the street to Donovan's Tavern.

There was a handwritten sign on the door that said the place was closed for a private party. As he climbed the concrete step he could hear the sound of voices and the Clancy Brothers on the jukebox. The wake was in full swing. As he pulled the door open he came face to face with Dan Brennan, Whitey's eldest son. He was probably posted there to keep the extreme riffraff out.

"Tommy, good to see you," Dan said, offering Tom his large, calloused hand.

"Hey Dan. How are you?"

"Fine, Tom. Sorry for your loss."

Tom had prepared himself for this, and with all the earnestness he could muster, replied, "Thank you."

Every stool at the bar that ran along the right side of the front room was occupied, as were the tables in the front room. It looked like it was standing room only in the back room, the place where Hugh had held court for years. Tom gave himself a moment for his eyes to adjust to the dim smoke filled room and find a familiar face.

Bonnie, the sixty something barmaid with the peroxide blond hair, was at her station behind the bar pulling a draft. Tom caught her eye and she smiled at him. She was dressed in black today and he could tell by her red-rimmed eyes that she had been crying.

"Tommy! Over here lad," Whitey's voice boomed from the far end of the bar. Whitey was standing with his other son, Pete and another rough looking guy that Tom had seen somewhere before. Tom made his way to them.

"You remember Jack O'Neill, don't ya?" Whitey said. Tom shook O'Neill's hand and said, "I don't think we've actually officially met."

O'Neill smiled wryly and then became serious. "Sorry for your loss, Tom."

"Thank you Jack."

O'Neill looked at Whitey and said, "Well, I'll be off. Sorry I can't stay longer." And then to Tom, "It was good to meet ya." And then, another almost imperceptible smile.

After Tom watched O'Neill make his way to the door, he turned to Whitey and said, "I swear I've seen that guy before."

"Yeah," Whitey said signaling to Bonnie. "He said you rousted him and a few of his friends on Chippewa about ten years ago after they got tossed out of a club."

Tom looked at Whitey, "He remembered that?"

"Sure, he said the only reason he didn't take a swing at ya is he knew Hugh was your granddad."

"Is that right?" Tom shook his head. Early on in his career as a cop he had had to stare down all kinds of drunks and reprobates. He was past the point now of caring to show some lowlife who owned the bigger set of balls.

"Sorry about Hugh, Tom." It was Pete Brennan.

Another somber reply from Tom, "Thanks Pete, I'm sure he'll be missed."

Whitey must have picked up on something because he shot Tom a dirty look. He turned to Bonnie who was now standing in front of them and said, "Bottle of Jameson dear, and two glasses."

Bonnie caught Tom's eye and looked at him sadly. Tom nodded to her and asked her, "How you holding up?"

"Alright Tommy. The place won't be the same without him."

"True, but as long as you're here it's still Donovan's," Tom replied.

Bonnie smiled and turned to get the bottle for Whitey. "Good turnout." Peter said, breaking the silence.

Tom looked around the bar and said, "Half of them probably want to make sure the old man is really dead."

That earned him another withering look from Whitey, who then shook his head and said, "You and he had a lot more in common than you think."

Tom put his hands up. For all that Hugh had meant to him, he obviously meant something else to the people here at the bar. He decided to stow his cynicism for the time being. Whitey picked up the bottle and the glasses and looked directly at Tom.

"I'm glad you came lad. I was hoping you and I could have a talk."

Tom looked at the bottle and said, "Um... okay."

"Upstairs, in the office," Whitey said. He looked at Pete and added, "Keep an eye on these knuckleheads, would ya?"

"Sure pop."

They went up the side stairwell to the "office." It had originally been the home of Tom's great grandfather who had bought the bar with the money he had made running liquor across the Niagara River and Lake Erie during prohibition. Later, it served as the center of Hugh's book making operation; satellite dish, color televisions, ticker tape machine and all. After the state of New York and the Indians made illegal bookmaking obsolete, it was turned into an office. As Hugh got older and had trouble mounting the steep staircase it was used mostly for storage. The only vestige of its former lives were and old tube RCA T.V. and a desk, in what used to be the sitting room.

Whitey took one of the two seats in front of the desk and motioned Tom to the other one. He uncapped the bottle and poured a glass, neat. He motioned with the bottle towards the other glass and looked at Tom with a raised eyebrow.

"Ah…" Tom trailed off. He had lost his taste for liquor since his last concussion. For several months he had headaches and bouts of light-headedness. He had been symptom free for a while but the thought of drinking still didn't appeal to him, especially straight Irish whiskey.

"Just one Tom," Whitey implored. "One last toast to the old man?"

"Alright."

Tom sat down and took the glass that was offered to him. "To Hugh," Whitey said.

"To Hugh." As Tom said it he felt something strange. Was it grief? He had seen Hugh a few times during the last few months of his life. It hadn't been easy. Hugh's cancer had at first made him more irritable that ever. Then later, his body and mind rapidly shut down to the point where he was very seldom cognizant of what was going on around him. Tom had done what he thought was the right thing but at the same time felt like he was just going through the motions. On the surface he was fine, deep inside he wasn't so sure.

They sat in silence for a while, taking small sips of the whiskey. Tom realized he would have to limit himself to one. He could already feel the effects. Whitey finally broke the silence.

"Tom," he started and then stopped.

"What is it, Whitey?"

"I don't know how to say this." Tom noticed that Whitey looked deeply concerned and couldn't seem to maintain eye contact.

"Jesus, Whitey, spit it out," Tom implored.

"I don't know what you expected to happen when your granddad passed but..."

Tom shook his head and smiled. "But what?" he asked.

"Well, with the bar and all."

Tom laughed and said, "I assumed that you would get the bar."

Whitey looked stunned. His mouth opened but nothing came out.

Tom, still smiling went on, "Is that what this is about? Of course, you would take over the bar. What the hell would I do with a tavern in South Buffalo?"

"Well, it's just that you being Hugh's last surviving heir and all."

Tom shook his head. "Whitey, you were more like family to Hugh than I ever was."

Whitey shook his head and pondered that for a moment. "To a point, Tom. But you have to know that the old man loved you. I know he didn't show it too often. And I'll be the first to admit that he could be a rotten prick, but he loved you."

Tom smiled again and nodded. "No arguments there. We were different." Whitey started to protest. "At least in some respects. I know he was a product of this neighborhood, this town and the Donovan gene pool. He was who he was."

Whitey thought for a moment and then said, "So you're alright with this?"

"For God's sake yes," Tom said, raising his glass. "You've stood by the family for all these years Whitey. It should go to you."

He clinked his glass with Tom and said, "That's very kind of you, Tom. God bless you."

"Did you see Hugh's will?" Tom asked.

"No, but Hugh mentioned it a while back. He said to make sure you knew why and that you wouldn't be forgotten."

Tom wondered what that meant. "There was a will wasn't there?"

Whitey poured himself another glass and didn't argue with Tom when he declined a refill. He set the bottle down and said, "Yes, his lawyer said it will be executed in a week or so."

"His lawyer?"

"Sid Ableson."

"Sid, Sid Ableson?" Tom asked incredulously. "He's still alive?"

Whitey chuckled and replied, "Barely. He's semi-retired but the old man stuck with him for all these years because he fit all of his requirements."

"Which were?"

Whitey counted them off on his thick fingers. "He was tough, he was discreet and he was Jewish."

"Of course." Tom nodded.

Tom politely stayed at the tavern for another hour, accepting condolences and listening to stories about Hugh. Most of them he had heard before and he knew many of them had been embellished. Who was he to tamp down on this outpouring of emotion? Let them have their memories. Finally he left and made his way back to his apartment on St. James, stopping to grab a sandwich at the pizza place around the corner on Delevan.

He gathered up his jacket, tie and food and walked the half block from his parking space to the front steps of the house on St. James where he rented the upper flat. As he opened the lower door, he heard a commotion from the downstairs flat. There was a crash and the sound of footsteps running away.

"Brandon!" It was the voice of Tom's downstairs neighbor, Caroline. She had lived in the lower flat since before Tom had moved in upstairs. She had explained to Tom that her son, Brandon had

Asperger's syndrome, and even though he was highly intelligent and basically a good kid, the Asperger's had caused some behavioral issues.

"Brandon!" Her front door was partially open and Tom could hear an unusual strain in her voice. Caroline was a single mother. She worked full time and devoted whatever time was left to her son. Tom knew her to be extremely patient with Brandon's quirks and was doing her best to help him lead a normal life. He had never heard her sound so desperate. He hesitated for a moment in the foyer and then pushed her door open and stepped into the living room. He saw that the coffee table was on its side; that must have been the crash.

"We have to go!" Her voice came from the back of the apartment. Tom hesitated for a moment. He didn't want to intrude in a family matter, but there was something in Caroline's inflection that made him think that something serious was happening. He walked to the doorway between the living room and the kitchen and cleared his throat.

"Caroline." He tried to say it at such a volume that he could be heard without startling her. There was silence for a moment and then she appeared in the doorway that lead from the kitchen to the hallway and the bedrooms. There was a mix of anger and nervousness on her round, pretty face and tears were streaming down her cheeks. She had on black slacks and a light blue sweater. She looked confused as she looked his way, as if wondering who would enter her apartment. Her face relaxed ever so slightly as her mind seemed to catch up.

"Tom?" was all that came out.

"Caroline... what's going on? Are you okay?"

She was obviously trying to calm herself down and slow down her breathing. She wiped a tear away and just looked at him.

"I'm sorry," Tom said. "I didn't mean to barge in. It just sounded..." he paused, trying to read her.

She shook her head. "No, no, it's alright. It's just I have a family emergency and now Brandon has locked himself in his room."

Tom was at a loss for a moment and then went with the only thing he knew. "Is there anything I can do?"

Caroline was rubbing her temples with her fingertips. "I need to get to St. Joseph's Hospital."

"What's going on?"

"It's my brother. He's been there for over twelve hours and they only now got a hold of my dad. They say it looks like he got mugged."

Tom kept his voice calm and empathetic. "Is he hurt badly?"

"Unconscious since they brought him in, that's all my dad told me and then he left for the hospital."

Tom looked over he shoulder down the hallway toward the bedrooms. Suddenly, he figured it all out. "And Brandon won't leave?"

Caroline's eyes misted up again. She inhaled and grimaced. "I can't leave him alone and I can't take him with me."

"Go," Tom said. "I can stay with him."

A tear rolled freely down her cheek. "I can't ask you to do that Tom."

He smiled at her, picked a paper napkin off the holder on the table and handed it to her. "Sure you can. I was a cop for ten years. I think I can handle a ten year old."

"But he's not your typical ten-year-old."

"I know. But I can stay here until you get to the hospital and see what's going on. If I have any questions I'll call you."

She bit her lower lip and thought about it. Finally she nodded. "Okay, but the first sign of trouble, you'll call?"

Tom nodded. "Understood," he said. "Are you going to be okay to drive?"

She straightened up and wiped her eyes with the napkin. She didn't wear much make-up but she had managed to smudge what she had on. "Yeah. Now that I know Brandon will be okay." She walked up to Tom and hugged him. "Thank you, Tom," she said, pressing her body to his.

"No worries. Just go and be careful."

"I will. There's food in the fridge, when, or if, he comes out," she said with one last glance over her shoulder towards the back. She blew her nose and took her keys off the counter and left.

"Now what?" Tom thought to himself. He stood in the kitchen for a moment and then went down the hall. He knew from his conversations with Caroline that Brandon's room was directly under the room in his flat where he had his speed bag mounted. The door to Brandon's room was closed and when Tom stopped he could hear a rhythmic knocking coming from inside and nothing else. He stood outside the door and thought about his next course of action as a nanny in training.

Chapter 3

Tom stood for a moment outside of Brandon's room until the knocking stopped and it fell totally silent. He raised his hand to knock on the door but then hesitated. In the six years he had lived above Caroline and Brandon Krupp he had only spoken to the boy a handful of times. Caroline had explained that her son had issues communicating with others. He tended to avoid eye contact and their conversations were very literal, no embellishments, exaggerations or any deviations from the factual. Tom wasn't sure exactly what he would say to Brandon if he did answer the door, so he took a step back. The silence was becoming unnerving until he heard the boy's voice, muffled through the door as it was, start to speak in a flat even tone. It sounded like he was reading. Tom relaxed and retreated to the kitchen.

It was almost 6:00 PM. Tom still hadn't eaten anything since before the funeral. He remembered he had set the bag with his sandwich on the steps in the hallway. He retrieved it and went back to the kitchen. The late afternoon air was starting to feel closed in the small flat so he opened one of the kitchen windows letting in a slight breeze. He unwrapped his sandwich and realized he needed something to wash it down. He thought about running upstairs to grab a bottle of water but didn't think he should leave. He went over to the refrigerator and looked inside.

There was some soy milk, some kind of diet shake and a bottle of apple juice. The apple juice was probably the least unappealing, so he grabbed that and started to look for a glass in one of the cabinets.

"That's mine," came a small voice from behind him. Tom turned around and saw Brandon standing in the doorway.

"Oh..." he said, looking at the bottle. "I didn't know."

"You can have some."

"Thanks," Tom said. "Would you like some?"

"No."

Tom poured himself a glass and sat down at the table. He knew the boy was watching him out of the corner of his eye.

"Where is Mom?" Brandon asked flatly.

Tom looked at him now. "She went to see your uncle..." he realized he didn't know the uncle's name.

"Mark."

"Right, your uncle Mark. I guess he's in the hospital."

Brandon looked down at his feet. "She wanted me to go, but I didn't want to."

Tom thought about asking him why, but decided not to. "Are you hungry?" he asked instead.

Brandon focused on the wrapped sandwich in front of Tom. "Yes. What is that?"

"Turkey sub. Would you like some?"

Brandon hesitated and then said, "I don't like turkey."

Tom just looked at the boy who was gripping the hem of his t-shirt nervously. He was starting to think that maybe he had taken on too much. "What do you like to eat?"

"I like applesauce." Tom noticed that the boy's voice was almost completely without intonation.

Tom started to get up to look for applesauce but Brandon had already stepped over to the refrigerator and began to open it. Brandon took out a single serving container of applesauce and then a spoon from one of the drawers. He sat down across the small kitchen table from Tom. Tom started to unwrap his sandwich but saw Brandon was just sitting there looking at the table. "Do you want me to open it for you?" he asked.

"Yes."

Tom reached over and took the container, peeled off the lid and set it down on the table. Brandon hopped up out of his chair and picked up the lid and threw it in the garbage receptacle next to the refrigerator. He then went back to his seat. "Mom likes to keep the kitchen clean," he said.

"That's good," was all Tom could come up with as a reply. They started eating in relative silence, the sound of birds' chirping coming in from the open window.

After a while, Tom's curiosity got the better of him. "Brandon, can I ask you a question?"

The boy looked up, not quite meeting Tom's eyes, but looking at Tom's chin. "Okay," he said.

"What was that knocking I heard coming from your room before?"

Brandon looked away again, focusing on his snack. When he didn't reply right away Tom thought that maybe he had crossed a line and embarrassed the boy. After a few more moments though Brandon replied, "When I get mad, sometimes I sit on my bed and rock."

"Oh. I was just wondering."

"Is that what you do?" Brandon asked.

Tom was puzzled. "What I do?"

"I hear you upstairs sometimes. The room above mine. There is a thumping sound."

Tom understood and smiled. "That's a punching bag. I guess I use that when I get mad."

Brandon processed this and then asked, "Are you a fighter?"

"I used to be."

"MMA?" Brandon asked, referring to Mixed Martial Arts, a sport that had supplanted boxing in the public imagination. Tom saw MMA fighting as a sort of loosely organized street fighting with very few rules and almost none of the mental aspect that he had found in boxing. But it was all the rage now and Tom did admit he respected the commitment and the fearlessness that the fighters showed.

"I used to be a boxer."

"Oh," Brandon said, looking disappointed. "I watch MMA."

"Yeah?"

"Mom doesn't like it but I do." He got up from his chair, threw out the empty container and rinsed off his spoon. Then he ran out of the room. Tom looked after him wondering what had just happened when Brandon came back with a notebook.

"What's that?" Tom asked.

"I keep statistics on my favorite fighters."

"Can I see it?"

Brandon clutched the notebook tightly and said, "No."

Tom didn't know what to do with that so he just cleaned up his place and threw away his wrapper. Brandon hadn't moved so Tom just returned to his seat and waited.

"I want to be an MMA fighter," Brandon finally said.

"That's cool," Tom answered.

"I want to beat up some kids at school."

"Take it from me pal, you don't want to get in fights at school. You can get in a lot of trouble."

Brandon frowned and looked down at the floor again. He quietly said, "Not a lot of fights. Just the kids who call me spaz and robot boy."

Tom's heart sank a little bit. He remembered from his youth how the "special" kids had been ostracized and mocked. He had never taken part, but then again he had never known any of them personally, until now. He thought for a moment and then said, "I can't teach you MMA, but I could show you how to hit the bag." Brandon said nothing, but his gaze shifted over to Tom's feet. Tom went on, "I don't want you to go around punching people, but it does help me when I feel frustrated." After a moment, Brandon nodded and they headed upstairs.

At first Tom thought that he had made a mistake. Caroline had described Brandon as being a little awkward due to the Asperger's, but the boy was downright uncoordinated. Tom gave him a quick tutorial and then put him on a chair so he could reach the bag, standing right behind him in case he lost his balance. Brandon seemed to be aware of his limitations though and fought off any self-consciousness he was feeling. He swung awkwardly at the bag and missed a few times. But he was focused and seemed to be lost in the satisfaction of hitting out at an inanimate object.

Brandon stopped suddenly after about twenty minutes and said, "My hand hurts."

Tom looked at the boy's right hand. It was red and a little swollen. "We'll put some Ice on that." He helped Brandon down from the chair and said, "We'll have to get you some gloves."

For the first time he saw a trace of a smile on the boy's face. They moved to Tom's living room and found a MMA fight on one of the sports' channels. Tom made some popcorn and Brandon seemed perfectly content to sit quietly and watch the fights seated next to Tom on the couch.

Caroline called once at about 8:30 to check in. Tom heard the strain in her voice and tried to calm her down. "We're fine," he said. "Don't worry about us." He told her they were in his apartment, just hanging out. "We'll see you when you get home." She hadn't added anything about her brother, but Tom sensed that the news wasn't good.

<<<>>>

There was a knock on the door that woke him up. Tom felt something by his side, and found Brandon leaning against him, sound asleep. He carefully moved the boy over and got up. He looked at his watch; it was just after midnight. He turned off the TV and went to the door.

She must have washed her face at the hospital because it was now make-up free but her eyes were red rimmed from crying. She tried to smile but it didn't take.

"Sorry," Tom said through his dry mouth. "I meant to take him downstairs but we fell asleep."

"Don't worry about it," she said, trying the smile again. "I'm just so grateful that you did this for us."

Tom stepped aside and Caroline entered the room and looked over at her son. She seemed to be trying to decide what to do when Tom interceded. He stepped over to the couch and picked Brandon up and carried him downstairs to his room. Caroline spent a few minutes in Brandon's room getting him ready for bed and then came out and joined Tom in the kitchen. She looked slightly more composed.

"Coffee?" she asked.

"No thanks."

She had already taken the bag of coffee out of the cupboard and said, "Are you sure, I'm going to make some anyway."

There was something in her tone that told Tom that she had something she wanted to get off her chest. In the time that he had known her she had never been one to drop her problems on him despite all of the challenges she faced. She was one of the most positive people he knew. This was different somehow. "Well, sure. If you're going to have some."

She had been speaking barely above a whisper and now she said, "Why don't you grab a seat in the living room and I'll bring it out. Is soy milk OK?"

"Black is fine."

A few minutes later Caroline came in with two mugs of coffee and sat down opposite Tom who had seated himself in a high backed arm-chair. She closed her eyes and exhaled.

"How's your brother?" Tom asked after a moment.

"Not good. He's in a coma."

"Jesus, Caroline. What happened?"

"There was a detective at the hospital. He said it looked like Mark got mugged."

"Where?"

She dabbed at her eyes with a wadded up tissue that had been clenched in her fist. "They found him by the foot bridge at the edge of Cheektowaga Town Park."

Tom thought for a moment. The ex-cop in him was always curious by nature, and he sometimes still had to remind himself he no longer carried a badge. There were questions that he wanted to ask but held off.

Caroline sniffled and then said, "They found him this morning, no wallet, no cell phone. It took them all day to identify him. They found him laying in the creek bed with his head split open."

Tom winced a bit and he felt a slight pain on the back of his head where he had been struck some time ago. He wrote it off as being psychosomatic and went on. "What do the doctors say?"

"They don't know." She stopped to blow her nose. "There's a lot of fluid and swelling on his brain..." she let go and started crying full out. Tom moved over to the couch and put his hand on her arm. He tried to think of something to say but came up empty.

She stopped sobbing and dried her eyes again with what little was left of the tissue, took a few breaths and said," The worst part is that when or if... he comes out of it he is going to be in trouble."

"What do you mean?"

She looked at him. "The detective said that it looks like Mark was violating the order of protection that his wife has on him."

"Shit. Really?"

She nodded. They have an apartment on David Avenue, or had until she kicked him out. They said it looked like he was stalking her."

Tom was starting to regret asking, but his neighbor seemed extremely distraught. He had seen his share of domestic disputes in his time and they were almost always emotionally wrenching.

"Caroline, I'm so sorry."

"It doesn't make sense," she interrupted.

"What doesn't?"

Her voice was breaking, but now there was anger in it. "He would never do that. He had been talking to a lawyer about getting custody of his daughter. He would never jeopardize that."

Well shit, Tom thought, there's a kid involved too. "Why would he be in the park?"

"I don't know. It just doesn't make any sense. And the order of protection is bullshit anyway." She was struggling to hold herself together. "His wife is an unstable, manipulative bitch. She attacked him and he pushed her off. She fell and sprained her wrist so she had him arrested. They didn't even care about the scratches on his face."

Tom put his arm around her and she buried her damp face into his shoulder. They sat like that for a while until Caroline stopped crying again. A wave of exhaustion washed over Tom. "I'll tell you what, if you want, I can make a few phone calls, see what's going on."

She sat up and composed herself again. "You don't have to do that."

"It's alright. I know a couple of the Cops in Cheektowaga and I work for a couple of blood thirsty lawyers."

"I wouldn't ask you to..." her voice trailed off.

"It's not a problem. What did you say the Detectives name was?"

She thought for a moment and then said, "Nightingale. And be careful. My dad almost took a swing at him at the hospital."

Tom smiled and stood up. "I'll tread lightly," he said.

She stood and smiled; this time it seemed genuine. "Thank you Tom. And thanks again for watching Brandon."

"We had a good time," he said. "And what are neighbors for?"

She hugged him tightly around his neck and then they separated, a little self-consciously.

"I'll let you know if I find anything out." He turned and let himself out and then went up to his apartment.

Chapter 4

Donovan was wide awake at 6:15 with the thought of Caroline's brother foremost on his mind.

He knew next to nothing about Mark Krupp; he could be an innocent victim, a piece of shit wife beater or somewhere in between. Caroline had enough intelligence and common sense though not to mistake family loyalty for the truth. There could be more to the story than the official version.

He knew that she put Brandon on the bus at 8:15. He had some time to kill so he headed to the gym. After he had recovered from his concussion sufficiently he gradually got back into working out. He mostly did it at the gym. He had discovered, as he was a few months shy of his fortieth birthday that running on sidewalks and pavement bothered his knees so he headed indoors. He was back at the apartment just before eight and he knocked on Caroline's door. He had a few follow up questions that he had thought of while he was on the elliptical machine.

Caroline looked much better. She explained that she was taking a personal day to spend time at the hospital. She still seemed agitated while talking about Mark's situation, but looked like she was ready to move on and take care of herself and Brandon. Brandon actually smiled at Tom as he brushed past on his way out the door when the bus pulled up.

He went upstairs and called the number for the Cheektowaga police and left a message for Detective Nightingale. Nothing too long, just a request for a call back. After a shower he wiped off the mirror and looked at himself. Without the road training he had done since he was a teenager he had put on about fifteen pounds, most of it muscle. He had let his dark hair grow out from the close-cropped style he had worn as a policeman. He was a civilian now; it was one of his attempts at trying to let go. It was by no means what you would call long, but it now showed the gray flecks and streaks that also meant he was getting older. The circles under his green eyes were almost gone. There was a feeling that had been creeping up on him lately that he couldn't put his finger on, some type of inner calm.

Professionally, he still felt he was not quite where he wanted to be. After Frederickson and

Associates was dissolved he had kept his PI license up to date and did work for Bob Stanley, the attorney who had helped him through his legal troubles a few years before, and Stanley's partners. He had also landed a job with a security firm that kept him fairly busy. He was one of the first ones the owner called for important jobs because of his experience and his gun carry permit. He had mixed feelings about carrying the gun when it was required. He liked the familiar feeling of security that the weight of the 9 mm Glock on his hip gave him, but the thought of using it still made his stomach churn. In his ten years as a policeman he had only fired his weapon in the line of duty on one occasion, but on that one occasion he had killed two men and lost his job. He wasn't getting rich, but he was paying his bills and saving up for a down payment on a replacement for the twelve year old Chevy.

Bob Stanley called while he was getting dressed. He wanted Tom to interview some potential witnesses for an upcoming trial to see if they would be fit to be deposed. Tom agreed and Stanley said he would e-mail the file to him. Tom booted up his laptop and printed out the attachment Stanley had sent. It looked like pretty standard stuff, a brief rundown of the case, an assault charge, and the names and contact information for five potential witnesses as well as a list of questions Stanley though were relevant. He and Tom had a good working relationship, with the understanding that Tom could go off script if he thought it would be useful. Stanley had complete confidence in Tom's instincts and he and his partners had been throwing a lot of work Tom's way.

Tom checked his watch; it was 9:30. He could start calling the five people now but then he thought about Caroline and her brother. What would be the harm of doing a little poking around? He went to his room and finished getting dressed. He put on a pair of dark pants and a blazer over a gray button down shirt. He had found that "business casual" gave him a little more professional gravitas than jeans and a sweatshirt.

Twenty-five minutes later he turned off of Harlem Road into the north entrance of Cheektowaga Town Park. He had printed a map of the park before he left his apartment and knew where he was going. The air was mild and a hazy sun was shining as he got out of the car and walked down the path towards the footbridge. He got to the foot of the bridge and took the map out of his jacket pocket. He looked to the right of the bridge and then the left. The left side must have been where they found Mark Krupp. The grass was trampled and there were foot prints everywhere and as Tom got closer he saw what he thought were probably wheel prints from an EMS gurney. Even if he was a policeman with a forensic unit at his disposal the scene was a mess and would probably yield nothing as far as what had happened two nights before. He looked at the map and the area on the other side of the bridge. He had circled the approximate location of the apartment Mark had shared with his wife and daughter and figured that Mark would have more then likely been in violation of the court order.

Detective Nightingale still hadn't returned his call. He might be working a later shift or maybe he had just disregarded the message. Tom considered calling again but then decided that since he was already in Cheektowaga he would just drive to the police station and try to get a face-to-face. He turned around to make his way back to his car.

A dark blue police cruiser was driving slowly through the park. Tom couldn't see for sure, but he sensed he was being given a good looking over. How many times had he done the same thing himself? Of course, that was in some of Buffalo's roughest neighborhoods, not in a grassy park on a warm spring day. The police car slowed for a moment and then when Tom kept walking towards it the cop accelerated ever so slightly, drove to the entrance and made a right onto Harlem.

Tom pulled into a visitor's space at the police station and went to the front entrance. On the right side of the lobby there was a window with inch thick Plexiglas and a bored looking officer seated behind it. Tom stood in front of the window until the man looked up from his computer screen.

"Can I help you, sir?" the officer asked in a monotone.

Tom took out a business card and pushed it through the slot at the bottom of the window. "I was wondering if Detective Nightingale was in?"

The heavyset man behind the window frowned slightly at the card. After a moment he said, "And may I ask what this is pertaining to?" Clearly he had taken on the roll of gatekeeper.

Tom was making every effort to be positive and professional. He knew he would get nowhere if he aggravated the man. "It's about a mugging that happened in the park the other night."

The man looked from Tom back to the card and pursed his lips. Tom imagined he was trying to think of a way to give him the brush off.

Suddenly a tall, middle-aged man walked up next to the officer from around a corner. He had salt and pepper hair, cut short and was wearing a tan sport coat over a white golf shirt. The officer gave him Donovan's card and went back to his computer. The man in the sport coat also frowned at the card and then looked up at Tom. "Hang on, I'll be right out," he said.

Tom had gotten used to the standard police reaction to dealing with a P.I. Most cops thought of them as wannabe cops or low life operators whose only purpose was sticking their noses in other people's business. That's how he saw them when he was a cop, why would they be different?

A moment later a door off to the side buzzed and then clicked open. The man in the sport coat walked up to Tom and said, "I'm Nightingale."

Tom considered offering to shake hands, but Nightingale's body language told him this wasn't going to be a cordial visit. He cut to the chase. "Detective, I was wondering if I could ask you a couple of questions about Mark Krupp."

"And what is your interest in Mark Krupp?"

Tom had to tread carefully or he knew Nightingale would shut him down on the spot.

"His sister is concerned about him."

Nightingale looked at his watch as a sardonic smile spread across his face. "Look, Donovan, I was just heading out. What is it you want to know?" As he said it, he started to move towards the entrance.

Tom kept pace and said calmly, "She doesn't believe he would have violated the order of protection without good reason."

They were outside now, with the sound of traffic on Union Road rushing by. Nightingale looked aggravated. He turned on Tom and said "Tell your client that her brother is a bad boy. He pushed the mother of his child, who is half his size, down a flight of stairs. So the other night, when he appears to be out stalking, he gets his head caved in. A more cynical man than I would say that's a bit of Karma." He finished glaring at Tom and resumed his walk to the parking lot.

"Look, I agree it looks bad-"

"Good, I'm glad we agree on that," Nightingale cut him off. They had reached the side of an unmarked Ford and Nightingale looked at him once more. "I don't know what's worse, her sending you here, or you charging her for this bull shit."

Tom was unfazed but decided to back off a little. The guy was clearly not in the mood to entertain the thought that the incident in the park wasn't anything other than what it seemed.

"So it was just a mugging?"

"Yep," Nightingale said opening the car door. "Watch, wallet, cell phone, all taken. We found his car outside a bar across the street on Harlem. Looks like he was going to his old neighborhood through the park so no one would see his car. And then he got rolled."

"Have there been other muggings in the park?"

Nightingale shook his head and climbed into the car. He put his hand on the door handle and gave Tom what was supposed to be a final, withering look. "Look, Shamus, if you're looking for some scenario where your friend isn't some kind of wife beating scum bag, then good luck. That neighborhood around the park isn't what it used to be. Hell, we had a shooting in the park in broad daylight a couple of summers ago. That whole side of town hasn't been the same since we lost Schiller Park and Pine Ridge."

"What do you mean 'lost'?" Tom asked. He already knew the answer but wanted to hear the detective say it.

"You know. The neighborhood got a lot darker." With that Nightingale pulled his door shut and started the car. Tom stepped back before he had a chance to run over his foot.

To Tom, Nightingale's answer spoke volumes about his demeanor. He'd seen some veteran cops in the city get jaded as time went on and the job wore them down. He knew that the first ring suburbs had changed over the years as more and more people tried to leave the city's struggling neighborhoods. And with the new demographic came a fresh set of problems. Nightingale struck him as being inflexible and unimaginative. What if he was right though? What if it was just as it seemed? The only person saying otherwise was the victim's sister, who would, of course, be biased.

Tom had work to do, actual income generating work. He would have to tell Caroline the bad news that her brother, despite the fact that he was the one in intensive care, was in trouble.

It was almost two o'clock when he found a parking space across from his apartment. He'd been mentally preparing what he was going to tell Caroline but as he crossed the street he saw Caroline's father, Leonard, seated on the front steps. Lenny Krupp stood up as Tom approached. He looked like he hadn't slept last night.

Tom had met him a few times and they had a nodding acquaintance, more or less.

Tom offered his hand. "Mr. Krupp, I was sorry to hear about Mark. How is he?"

"The same, Tom. And thanks for what you did for Caroline yesterday."

"My pleasure," Tom said. The two men fell silent for a moment and then Tom looked at the open door to the foyer of his apartment. "Is Caroline here?"

Lenny looked over his shoulder and seemed to think of something. "No, she's at the hospital with her brother. I came here to pick up Brandon." He was staring at Tom as if waiting for something. When Tom didn't say anything and was about to move past him he finally spoke. "She said you might make a few calls on Mark's behalf."

"Yes, I did." Tom looked Lenny in the eye. "As a matter of fact, I went out to Cheektowaga and spoke to Detective Nightingale today."

Lenny frowned deeply and said, "That guy... what did he tell you?"

"Pretty much the same thing he told you and Caroline. Mark was in the wrong place at the wrong time."

Now Lenny shook his head. "That man has already made his mind up."

"Mr. Krupp–"

Lenny interrupted him. "There is no way Mark would have been within ten miles of that woman unless he thought his daughter was in danger. We had a lawyer and Mark was seeking custody."

Tom saw the distress rising in the other man. He didn't want to make things worse by feeding into it or dismissing it. He lowered his voice and asked, "Why would Mark think his daughter was in trouble?"

"That girl! His wife. She's a crazy, manipulative bitch!"

Tom nodded. He was hoping that he could let Lenny talk himself down. "Caroline has said as much. But I'm afraid, as Mark has probably been finding out, that the State of New York is slightly biased towards the mother."

"Don't I know it?" Lenny raised a finger, pointing it at nothing in particular. "The only reason they got married is the fact that she got knocked up. Hell if he hadn't been my own son I would have told him the baby probably wasn't his anyway!"

His words hung in the air for a moment and then Lenny flushed slightly and lowered his hand. He looked down at the ground and said, "I'm sorry Tom. I love my son and my granddaughter, but there's times I wish he'd never met Jenny."

"So the order of protection?"

Lenny looked up again and Tom wished he hadn't asked. The fire was back in his eyes. "The order of protection is bull shit! Mark came home one day after he'd found out she had emptied their checking account. He confronted her and she attacked him.

He still has the scars on his cheek from where she dug her claws into him. When he pushed her off she sprained her wrist. When the cops showed up all they had to do was look at the two of them and decide Mark was at fault."

"What do you mean?"

Lenny closed his eyes and continued, "Mark is a big kid. He's gentle as a lamb though. He's always been aware of his size and would never raise a hand to a woman. He was raised better than that. So, his wife gives the cops some sob story and Mark refuses to stick up for himself, and bingo, it's off to jail and out of his home."

Tom let Lenny calm himself down for a moment and then said, "Mr. Krupp, I can't promise you anything, but there are a few more avenues I could explore."

"We'll pay you, of course," Krupp said, quieter now.

Tom shook his head. "That won't be necessary."

Lenny started to protest but Tom waived him off. "It's just a couple of phone calls, that's all. I know a few people who might give us some advice."

Lenny exhaled and said, "Thanks Tom. Caroline was right. You're a good guy."

Tom smiled, shook Lenny's hand again and then went into the foyer. Lenny or Caroline had picked up the mail off the floor and put it on the small table that stood on the side of the foyer. Tom grabbed his and started up the stairs. It looked like the usual day's allotment of junk mail until he got to the envelope with the return address marked, *Sidney M. Ableson, Esq.* Tom opened the door to his flat, set the junk mail down and tore open the letter from the lawyer.

His grandfather's will would be read the following Monday. Ableson might be one step ahead of the reaper himself, but he was on the ball Tom thought. He put the letter on top of the rest of his mail.

Chapter 5

Tom spent the next couple of days running down Bob Stanley's list of potential witnesses with mixed results. He managed to arrange face-to-face interviews with three of them and ruled two of them out. The other two proved more elusive. He had spoken to a man named Metcalf on the phone who said he was there at the time that Stanley's client allegedly assaulted the man who filed the report, but he wasn't sure if he could recall it clearly. The incident had occurred at a bar on Chippewa and Tom guessed that Metcalf might have been three sheets to the wind himself. The fifth potential witness was a doorman at the club who had broken up the altercation and given the cops a very vague statement about what he saw. Tom had no luck locating the man with any of the contact information Stanley had supplied. Thursday night he typed up his preliminary report and emailed it to Stanley.

Shortly after seven PM he went downstairs and knocked on Caroline's door. She was still in her work clothes and Tom could smell the aroma of something cooking in the kitchen.

"Hi, is this a bad time?" he asked apologetically.

Caroline shook her head. "No we just got home a little while ago. We were about to eat. Would you like to join us?"

"No, thank you. I was just wondering how your brother was?"

Caroline's smile slipped away and Tom felt a twinge in his stomach. "He's still the same," she said. "No worse, but not any better either. They're still concerned about the swelling on his brain."

"Sorry to hear that," was all Tom could come up with when she paused.

Caroline glanced over her shoulder towards the kitchen and then back to Tom. "I heard my dad gave you an earful the other day," she said.

Tom smiled sheepishly. "He told me what he thought about the whole thing. I can understand why he would be upset."

Caroline bit her lower lip and seemed to be thinking of something. After a moment she asked, "He said you talked to the detective."

Tom decided not to sugarcoat it. "Yeah, he seems to have made up his mind."

She frowned now and looked down. Tom continued, "Look Caroline, I'll be honest. It looks like your brother violated the court order."

"I know," she said quietly.

"I told your father that there were a couple of other things that we can consider before we throw in the towel. I have an out of town job this weekend, but when I get back I'll pick it up again. The important thing now is that he gets better so he can give his side of the story."

She looked him in the eye and said, "I know... but even if he does, like you said, this Nightingale has made up his mind, so will it make any difference?"

Tom thought for a moment and then said, "Honestly, I don't know. But it's the best chance he has."

She grimaced when he finished and then composed herself. "Thank you Tom. Are you sure you're not hungry?"

Tom smiled. "No, thanks, I already ate," he lied. The truth was the smell of whatever she was cooking was making his mouth water. He felt like a heel but he needed to get out of there. He didn't know if he was helping matters any or just getting her hopes up. "I'll be back Sunday night. Let me know if there's any change with your brother."

"Okay," she said. The cloud seemed to have passed over her countenance. "Thanks again, Tom."

He went upstairs and thought about packing. He had drawn an assignment from Rod Barlow, the president of Barlow Security, to escort a jeweler named Milt Jasper to Albany for a gem show. Jasper was bringing a case with an undisclosed amount of inventory with him and had asked for an armed escort. Rod Barlow would have taken the job himself but his son had a baseball tournament and he asked Tom if he could cover. The job paid well, but Tom would have to be armed and on his toes.

As he walked upstairs to his flat an alarm went off in his head. He had told his mother he would have dinner with her and her... what would you call him, boyfriend? He had to pick up Jasper at his showroom at noon tomorrow to start the trip to Albany to make sure Jasper was safe and sound and registered for the show.

He dialed the number for his uncle's house and Sam's wife Dianne answered on the second ring. After finding out his mother was out he asked that Dianne have her call him as soon as possible. He almost asked Dianne if she knew anything about her mother's suitor but decided to let it be for the time being. He had an image of his sixty-three year old mother sneaking out of the house for the rendezvous to avoid her older brother's wrath and it made him shake his head and smile. He decided the less said the better, at least for the time being.

Tom's mother didn't get back to him until the following morning. She sounded genuinely disappointed but said she understood. Tom promised her that he would make it up to her next week. At eleven AM he went to Rod Barlow's office and picked up the "War Wagon," a tricked out, late model SUV that was twice the size of Tom's car and as far as he was concerned handled like an aircraft carrier. Barlow explained that it was more about image than security and his clients seemed to like it just fine.

The trip to Albany was uneventful. Tom learned more about precious stones from Milt Jasper than he thought was possible. Jasper was nice enough, but between his passion for his profession and the copious amount of aftershave he was wearing, Tom attempted to make the trip in record time.

They checked into a downtown hotel that was a short drive from the Javits Convention Center. After check-in, they locked Milt's valuables in the room's safe and ordered room service. Tom excused himself saying he wanted to be extra sharp in the morning and went to his room after assuring

Milt he would leave the door between their suites unlocked and his gun at the ready. The jeweler gave him a quizzical look and then laughed. He waved Tom off and said goodnight.

Chapter 6

Hector Arroyo was pissed. Not as angry as he had been when he left the warehouse with his tail between his legs; a few beers and a game of pool had helped, but he was still upset.

It hadn't been his fault that the pallet of non-dairy creamer hadn't been wrapped properly. When he felt the weight shift his attention lapsed for one split second and he hit a concrete pylon on the loading dock with his forklift.

They don't screw around anymore. There was mandatory drug testing for any workplace accident involving machinery. And no twenty-four hour window to report to the clinic for a piss test. No, no you go to the security office and the supervisor sticks the swab right in your mouth. He could swear the foreman was smiling through the whole thing. That pendejo had it out for him.

Now he had all weekend to worry about it. He knew there was a good chance nothing would show up. It had been a while since he had gotten high. But until it was resolved he was off the forklift and back in the giant freezer, picking stock. You could wear as many layers as you could find and still freeze your ass off.

Things were pretty shitty at home too. Idalys still hadn't come back from her mom's with the kids since their last fight. Now he was going home to an empty house. She didn't understand, he had a temper. No cops had ever come pounding on his old man's door when he went off. It was wrong. A man should be with his family and be master of his own domain.

The cool night air cut into the beery haze as he stepped out of the bar onto Niagara Street. An image flashed in his mind. His kids. They had looked so scared when he and Idalys were going at it. He rounded to corner onto Fargo Avenue where his car was parked. He was angry but he knew deep inside that he had to do something about it. He needed his family.

He fumbled for his keys and dropped them onto the street, cursed to himself and bent over to retrieve them. He was just about to put them into the lock when he heard an engine accelerate. It was impossibly close to . . .

The SUV hit him, knocking him over the hood of his own car. Bones were shattered on impact and he flew through the air like a rag doll.

He might have survived had he not landed on his head, breaking his neck. The SUV didn't even slow down. Its taillights disappeared around the corner.

A few porch lights came on from the nearby houses. A man came out of his front door in bare feet, saw the body with its impossibly twisted limbs and neck. He made a sign of the cross and went back to his house to call 911.

The first patrol car was there in five minutes. The two officers got out, a stocky black man in his mid-thirties and a tall blond woman in her late twenties. They trained their flashlights on the dead man.

"Shit," the man said.

Sherry Palkowski was a rookie with the Buffalo PD. As much as she had been mentally preparing herself for the eventuality of a sight like the one before her, her stomach still lurched at the it. She looked up and took a few deep breaths.

"You okay?" her partner asked.

"Yeah."

"I'll take a look around. You want to call it in?" His tone was neither patronizing nor dismissive. She appreciated that.

"Okay," she said. She took one more look at the body and then went back to the car.

Chapter 7

The rest of the weekend in Albany was uneventful. Saturday morning Tom escorted the jeweler to the gem show at 9:30 and left him there. The organizers had provided an ample amount of security for the event, leaving Tom with nothing to do but poke around downtown Albany for eight hours. At six o'clock he picked Jasper up and they went back to the hotel, secured Jasper's valuables, had room service brought up and watched a movie. Then Jasper, all business, said he had to be on his toes in the morning, so he turned in.

The next morning they checked out early and Tom dropped Jasper off at the Convention Center. He only had six hours to kill today since the show ended at four. He found a coffee shop with free Wi-Fi to check his mail and do some reading. His mind kept going back to Mark Krupp's predicament. He kept thinking that there was very little he could do for the Krupps, but Caroline was so distraught and adamant about her brother's innocence. He was staring off into space when he caught the eye of one of the girls behind the counter. She appeared to be giving him the 'don't you have anywhere to be?' look so he was thinking about getting up when Jasper called. It was only 2:30 but Jasper said that the show was essentially over and they could go. They were on I-90 back to Buffalo by 3:15

After returning Jasper and his goods to the showroom and accepting a hundred dollar tip (which he had half heartedly tried to refuse), he returned the SUV to Barlow's parking lot and was in the process of moving his belongings back to his own car when his phone buzzed, It was Sherry.

"What are you doing?" she asked.

"I just got back from a job in Albany."

"Do you want to grab a beer?"

Tom looked at his watch. It was pushing ten PM. He never slept well in hotels and this weekend had been no exception. Added to the five monotonous hours in the car with a jeweler and he was really looking forward to going to bed.

"I don't know..." he started

He heard her sigh and then she said, "Don't worry about it."

He noticed something in her voice that sounded off. Sherry wasn't the most demonstrative person in the world, but it sounded like something was bothering her. Besides he had only seen her a handful of times since she had started with the Buffalo PD. "Screw it," he said. "I've got nothing going on for the next couple of days."

"Are you sure? You sound tired."

"Sure I'm sure. Where are you?"

She chuckled softly and said, "I was about to ask you the same thing. I'm outside of your apartment with a six pack of Yuengling."

"Be there in ten."

Tom was getting out of his car on St. James when Sherry walked up to him. He stared at her for a moment.

"What?" she asked.

"Your hair…"

"Oh yeah," she said, running her fingers through it. As long as he had known Sherry, her hair had been down to her shoulders. She had cut off about four inches. "One of the girls at work told me it's a lot less tempting to grab if you're in a scuffle."

"Makes sense… nobody ever told me that."

"Even when you were rocking the mullet?" She held out a hand and took the garment bag with Tom's suit in it from him.

Tom smiled. "How old do you think I am?"

Upstairs Tom went into his room and threw his bags down on the bed. He put on jeans and a t-shirt and went through the kitchen for a bottle opener. "Do you want a glass?" he called out to the living room.

"Are you still washing them by hand?" she called back.

"Yeah."

"Pass."

He went to the living room. Sherry was perched on her usual spot on his couch. He handed her the opener and she popped two tops and handed a bottle to him. He sat down on the recliner across from her. It was then that he noticed how tired she looked.

"So, rough weekend?" he dove right in.

She looked at him quizzically at first and then she closed her eyes. There was something on her mind. "Yeah, kind of." Tom took a pull on his beer and waited. "Friday night there was a hit and run... a fatality."

Tom nodded. "Pretty bad?"

"Well yeah, the guy was DOA. They figure the driver must have been doing about fifty. On a side street no less."

Tom remembered his first dead body, a homeless veteran who had frozen to death in the shadow of the Central Terminal on Paderewski Drive. He remembered how you can tell yourself how tough you are but it's still going to get to you. There had been other dead bodies over the ten years he had been a cop. The worst ones were the kids, innocent lives that had ended usually through no fault of their own.

She sighed and put her head back. "The thing that's really weird is that I knew the guy."

"Shit, how well?"

"Not that well, bet well enough to dislike him."

Tom was puzzled. "What are you talking about?"

She looked back across at Tom and said, "Two weeks ago Dante and I responded to a domestic and this guy, Hector Arroyo, had kicked the crap out of his baby mama. Knocked out a tooth and blackened her eye. She got a few licks in of her own but she was outmatched in the end. All in front of their two kids, ages six and four. When we came in he turned on us and Dante had to restrain him. Real Macho man."

Tom thought for a moment. "And you feel..."

"Nothing," she said instantly. "After wanting to throw up at seeing the mangled corpse I haven't felt a thing."

She looked down at her beer bottle, which Tom noticed she hadn't taken a drink from yet. "It could be shock, at least a mild case," he offered.

She seemed to consider that and finally took a sip of her beer. "I thought about that. But I keep thinking that I should feel something. I mean the guy was a world class asshole, but did he deserve to be run down like a dog?"

"That's not for you to decide," Tom said.

"Is this going to be a 'Randomness of the Universe' lecture?"

Tom smiled slightly. "No, no lectures from me. I reluctantly gave up trying to figure out why things happen." Sherry just looked at him so he continued, "I guess what I'm saying is that, things do happen. You're going to have to learn to process them without letting them drive you crazy."

They fell silent for a moment and Tom thought about Mark Krupp, lying in a hospital bed, clinging to life, just because he was in the wrong place at the wrong time.

"Donovan?" Sherry said, bringing him out of his reverie.

"Sorry, I was just thinking about Caroline's brother."

Tom told Sherry the condensed version of Mark Krupp's assault. When he finished she raised her eyebrows and said, "Really? So that's two guys we know with a history of domestic violence cut down in a week."

Tom didn't know what she was getting at. "Well, Caroline and her father are saying something is off with the whole thing. Why?"

"Just a wild thought..." she hesitated.

"That they're related?"

"Crazy right?"

"Sort of. Two totally different, probably random occurrences."

They talked for a while longer and Sherry seemed to come out of her funk enough to realize Tom was dead on his feet. They promised each other they would get together the following weekend and she left.

As Tom lay in bed before he went to sleep he thought about Hector Arroyo and Mark Krupp. He knew it wasn't up to him to decide if Arroyo had got what he deserved, but he knew that if what Mark Krupp's family said about him was true, he did not. He couldn't let it go, not yet. He had one more person he wanted to talk to.

Chapter 8

The late morning air was warming on what looked like it was going to be another near perfect spring day. Tom ascended the front porch of the duplex on David Avenue in Cheektowaga and looked at the mailbox. The name Krupp was there on the left hand box, in stick-on reflective letters. He straightened his tie and rang the bell.

Through the glass he saw a woman descending the stairs and then she pulled the door open. She looked up at Tom expectantly.

"Ms. Krupp?"

She was a petite brunette with large dark eyes. She was wearing a white tank top and tight pink sweat pants. She looked at Tom impatiently and then shot a look at the open door at the top of the stairs. "Yes," she said, looking over her shoulder.

"Sorry to disturb you," Tom said, handing her a business card. "My name is Tom Donovan. I know this is a difficult time but I was hoping I could ask you a few questions regarding Mark's insurance."

Jenny Krupp looked thoroughly confused. She shot another look up the stairs and then to Tom, "Okay. C'mon up would you, my little girl is watching TV."

They entered the apartment and Tom saw the little girl, probably around two years old, playing on the living room floor. Jenny picked up the remote and turned down the volume. She looked at the card again and then back at Tom. She took on a concerned look. "Is Mark..." her voice trailed off.

"I was just at the hospital," Tom said. "Mark's condition is unchanged. There are just a few things we need to get straight regarding his policy just in case, God forbid, Mark is unable to go back to work."

A tear rolled down her pale cheek. She let out a sound like a sob. It was one of the most disingenuous things Tom had ever heard. Tom knew he had a preconception about Jennifer Krupp. He had to be careful.

The place reeked of cigarette smoke. Tom knew people had their vices, but with a toddler in the house? At least she made it look good. His eyes swept the room quickly and there was no sign of an ashtray. Jennifer picked up the girl and looked at Tom.

"Would you like some coffee?"

"No thank you Mrs. Krupp. Like I said, I know this is difficult, but I won't take a lot of your time."

"Call Me Jen," she said sitting on the couch. The little girl looked at Tom and buried her face in her mother's shoulder.

Tom sat across from them in an old armchair with worn out springs. He had filled an old leather valise he found in his closet with a few papers and a legal pad. He opened it and took out the legal pad. He'd made a few notes and written out a few questions to make it look good.

"I just need to double check a few things," Tom said removing a pen from his jacket pocket. I apologize in advance if some of this seems redundant Jen. We just want to make sure everything is in order."

Something on the muted TV must have caught the little girl's attention because she wriggled off of her mother's lap and went over to stoop in front of it. Jen folded her arms in front of her, looked at Tom and waited.

"Your maiden name?" he started.

"Tyson." She spelled it for him.

Tom asked a few more innocuous questions until she relaxed and sat back. This was what he had hoped for. That he could wade through the whole 'grieving wife' bit.

"I understand you and your husband are separated?"

She blinked and bit her lower lip. "We've been... having some problems," she said quietly.

"Not that that has any bearing at the moment," Tom said, nodding his head. "We just need to make sure we have the latest information.

Out of the corner of his eye Tom noticed the little girl had walked right up to the TV and was inches away from the screen. If Jen noticed she didn't say anything.

"How old is your daughter?" Tom asked.

Jennifer finally glanced at the child and said, "That's too close Lexie." The child didn't seem to hear her. She looked back at Tom and said, "She's two and a half." She cocked her head, looked at Tom's left hand and asked, "Do you have any kids?"

Tom blushed despite himself and said, "Um no. I'm not married."

She seemed to think about this and began looking around where she sat. After a moment she stood up and said, "Excuse me for a minute."

"Sure."

She stood up and walked out of the room slowly. Something about the way she moved struck Tom as some minor act of seduction. Or was he imagining it? She had a narrow waist and the skintight sweats accentuated her bottom.

Tom looked at Alexis, still inches away from the TV screen. He remembered his mother scolding his sister Colleen many times for doing the same thing.

Jennifer came back in a moment later with a smart phone in her hand. She sat back down on the couch and reached over and put the phone on the coffee table. When she did she seemed to make an effort to let Tom see down her shirt. Tom was looking at the phone and he had a thought.

"Ms. Krupp, when was the last time you spoke to your husband?"

She frowned and a crease spread across her forehead. She didn't answer for a moment and Tom wondered if he had gone too far too soon. He was trying to figure out how to get by the awkward silence when she finally said, "The night he got arrested."

Tom pretended to make a note. She was glaring at him now warily. She had seemed to drop the coquettishness and in doing so her entire demeanor seemed to change. Tom looked at her and thought he saw a simple girl, someone who had always tried to get by on looks and sex appeal. The kind of girl who looks good in the dim lights of a bar or nightclub. The problem with that is eventually the act wears thin.

"I see," Tom said. "And you know, when Mark recovers he will probably be charged with violating the court order?"

She seemed extremely wary now. As if on cue the little girl started crying about something, adding to the tension in the room. Jennifer reached over and picked up the phone, this time less suggestively. She sat up and asked, "I'm sorry, but what does that have to do with insurance?" As soon as she finished her question she started punching something into the phone.

"Oh, probably nothing," Tom said waving it off as thought it he hadn't asked.

Tears were rolling down Alexis' face but Jennifer made no move towards her to comfort her. Tom saw it as an out. "Well I won't keep you any longer. Feel free to call the agency if you have any questions." He gave a smile and stood up, gathering his things.

She had finally gotten up and picked up her daughter. The gesture almost seemed unnatural to her. "So, do I need to sign something?" she asked irritably.

Tom shook his head. "No, not yet. Hopefully Mark will make a full recovery and be able to support you and your daughter without any further difficulty." He smiled again and moved towards the door. He opened it and glanced back. Jennifer was reading something on her phone and holding the crying child awkwardly in her other arm. "Have a nice day." Tom said as he went out the door.

He walked down to his car, unlocked the door and climbed in. Jennifer Krupp seemed to be everything Caroline had said she was. Tom knew it was a first impression and there was an outside chance he had caught her on a bad day. But something about her detachment from her child and the plight of her husband set off a warning signal.

He was just about to turn the key in the ignition when he glanced in his driver's side mirror and saw the dark blue police car creeping up the street. He had a feeling that it wasn't a coincidence. The cop pulled up alongside his car, effectively blocking him in. Tom sighed and slowly got out of the car.

The cop was climbing out of the cruiser and seemed startled to see Tom standing there. He was in his late twenties and stood a couple of inches shorter than Donovan. He had broad shoulders and thick arms like a rugby player. His blond hair was cropped close, probably compensating for it thinning on top and he was wearing wrap around sunglasses.

"Good morning officer," Tom said. "What can I do for you?"

The cop walked up within about three feet of Tom. The metal nametag on his shirt said J. Seifert. He hooked his thumbs in his belt and said, "You can start with your name."

Tom raised his eyebrows. "Have I done something wrong?"

Seifert tried to look hard. "What are you doing here?" he said slowly.

"Visiting a friend."

Seifert smirked. "Are you some kind of smart ass?"

"No, just a private citizen minding his own business on a lovely spring day."

The smirk left Seifert's face. He took off the sunglasses and looked hard at Tom. "I'm going to ask you one more time. Who are you and what are you doing here?"

Jennifer's phone. Had she texted the cops? No, more than likely she had texted one particular cop. The one standing in front of him now. Had this muscle bound idiot fallen prey to her feminine wiles? He looked back in the direction of Jennifer's apartment and back at Seifert knowingly. Seifert made a face, held out his left hand and said, "Let me see some ID."

"I don't think so," Tom said.

Seifert looked stunned. He shook his head and started "Listen asshole–"

Tom cut him off, "No, this isn't New York City and as far as I know, Cheektowaga doesn't have a 'Stop and Frisk' policy. So if you don't mind moving your car..."

Seifert regained some of his gravitas. "Maybe I should take you in," he said.

"It would be great if you had some kind of probable cause," Tom said as he reached into his jacket pocket.

Seifert turned white and reached for the 9 mm on his belt. Tom held up his hands, revealing that he had taken out his phone. Seifert uncoiled and Tom flipped it open and started to punch in a number.

"What are you doing?" Seifert asked impatiently.

"I'll have my lawyer meet us at the station. And you can explain to him and your bosses why you picked up an unarmed civilian for no reason."

"Put the phone down," Seifert barked.

"Oh and maybe you can show them your phone and the text you got from Jennifer Krupp a few minutes ago."

Seifert turned white again. Tom had called his bluff and let him know that he had made the connection. They stood looking at each other for a few minutes. Tom knew he had to offer the kid an out to end the standoff.

"Look, I just was trying to clear up some stuff with Jennifer about Mark."

Seifert bristled at that, but Tom went on, "It looks like things are just what they seemed so I am all done here. I don't see a need to get your bosses and my lawyer involved, especially with what he charges an hour. How about we just forget the whole thing and I'll be gone and out of your hair."

Seifert looked angry, but he was thinking about it. He took the out but added a caveat, "Sure. But if I see you around here again, it won't be so easy. Understand?"

"Crystal clear Officer." Tom stepped back and got in his car, started it and waited for Seifert to move the police car. Seifert pulled up ahead and parked at the curb. Tom pulled out and gave the cop a little wave as he drove by. He was sure by now Seifert was running his plates. He made it to Pine

Ridge Road and in five minutes was on the Kensington Expressway headed back into the city.

It dawned on Tom that it was probably Seifert who had been giving him the eye in the park the previous week. He had only seen him in silhouette but he was pretty sure it had been him. He'd guessed right about the text from Jennifer to the cop too. Was Seifert just another guy she was stringing along? Or was there more to it?

Tom was driving down Delaware Avenue towards home when his phone buzzed. He pulled over and saw Whitey Brennan's number on the screen.

"Whitey, what's up?"

"Tommy, where you been, lad? You missed the reading of the will."

Tom hadn't thought about the reading since he dropped the letter from Hugh's lawyer on top of the rest of his junk mail. "Shit. Sorry Whitey. I got caught up in a job I've been working on and the time got away from me. What did I miss?"

He heard Whitey sigh and then say, "Could you stop by the bar Tom?"

Tom was slightly frustrated that Whitey wouldn't just give him the highlights over the phone, but there was something about Whitey's tone that stopped him from protesting. He looked at his

101

watch; it was approaching noon. "Yeah, I could go for a sandwich. I'll be there in a half hour."

"Thanks, Tom. Lunch is on me," Whitey said.

As it should be, Tom thought. Whitey was obviously going to break the news that Hugh had left Tom nothing or next to nothing. Not that Tom had expected to be rewarded for the years of seldom-interrupted acrimony he had shared with his late grandfather. He put his phone away and started out for the South side.

Chapter 9

Tom pulled up the curb in front of Donovan's Tavern and got out of the car. It had gotten considerably warmer and the air conditioner in his car was sketchy at best so he peeled off his jacket and tie and put them on a hanger in the back seat. The front entrance of the bar was propped open and Tom made his way into the awaiting darkness of the tavern.

After a moment his eyes adjusted and he saw that things still looked the same as always. A couple of old men at the bar, nursing drafts, gazing up at the television and Bonnie at her spot on a stool behind the bar. Then he saw Jack O'Neill, the man he had met the day of Hugh's funeral, at the end of the bar reading the *News*.

Bonnie was all smiles. "Tommy! How are you handsome?"

"I'm good Bonnie. How are you?"

For some reason her face fell a little. "I'm okay. What can I get for you?"

"Nothing right now. I'm here to see Whitey. Is he in the back?"

O'Neill looked up from his paper and asked, "Is he expecting you?"

That aggravated Tom. Who was this guy? "I didn't know I needed an appointment."

O'Neill smirked. "He just has a lot on his plate is all."

The two men glared at each other for a moment. Bonnie finally broke the ice. "He's upstairs sweetie. Just go on up."

That earned Bonnie a short disapproving glance from O'Neill. Tom turned to her and smiled. "Thanks, gorgeous." He turned and went out to use the side staircase to the apartment upstairs.

When he walked in, the first thing he noticed was that the front room had been cleaned out and organized. The desk had been dusted and there was a laptop, a small printer and a new phone on it.

"There you are." Whitey's voice came from the other entrance to the room. He was holding a steaming cup of coffee. He moved towards Tom and shook his hand. He was smiling but there was obviously something on his mind. "Coffee?" he asked.

"No, I'm good."

Whitey pointed Tom towards a seat in front of the desk, but this time he himself took the office chair behind it. Meet the new boss, Tom thought.

"I saw Jack O'Neill downstairs," Tom said.

"Ah, yes," Whitey nodded. "Jackie's been doing a few odd jobs for us."

Tom smiled ruefully. "So, is he the new Whitey?"

Whitey chuckled. "Maybe. But that doesn't make me the new Hugh."

Tom nodded and said, "There was only one Hugh." He pointed at the electronics on the desk and asked, "What's all this stuff? Are you taking the bar into the last century?"

"You know how your granddad felt about technology. Dan and Peter set this up and installed some kind of record keeping program." Whitey frowned at the computer. "It's supposed to save time, but right now I'm afraid I'm all thumbs."

They fell quiet and Whitey's face became serious. He was looking down and Tom knew he was probably looking for a way to break the expected news about Hugh's will.

"What is it Whitey?" Tom asked. "Is this about the will?"

Whitey looked up and said, "Well, yes. Partially."

Tom prompted him, "Go on. Was it what we expected?"

Whitey nodded. "Mostly. As we discussed, he left the bar to me."

Another pause. No surprises yet, but Tom had the feeling he was going to have to drag the rest out of him. "Okay," he said.

Whitey looked at him sadly. Tom was fighting the urge to jump over the desk and shake his friend. "Whitey, it's okay. I didn't really expect anything."

"You shouldn't judge the man so harshly, Thomas," Whitey said defensively. "He did leave you something."

Tom looked around the room as he thought of what it could possibly be and then asked, "The house?"

Whitey closed his eyes and shook his head. "No... the house was put on the market to settle a little matter of back taxes your granddad had with the state."

Tom didn't really care about the house. It held no special memories for him. Besides Hugh, whom Tom was often at odds with, the only other recollection he had of the place was his late grandmother, who in the best of times was a stern, humorless woman. As she reached her seventies and senility set in she became even more unpleasant to be around. Tom did feel a pang of guilt for not seeing her in the few years before she died. His and Hugh's initial falling out had severely limited any chance of normal family relations.

Tom didn't dare say anything for fear of sounding flippant. He didn't want to upset Whitey any further. He simply nodded and waited for Whitey to go on.

"He left you the boat," Whitey finally said.

The boat was a 1929 Chris Craft that Tom's great grandfather had allegedly used to smuggle Canadian Whiskey across the Niagara River during prohibition. In his entire lifetime, Tom couldn't remember his grandfather ever putting the boat on the water. As far as he knew it had been in mothballs for decades. His first reaction was to ask what the hell was he supposed to do with a dilapidated boat, but he bit that off and simply said, "Oh..."

"I know it doesn't seem like much Tommy, but for some reason that old relic meant a lot to Hugh," Whitey offered. "He never talked about it and I think the only time he saw it recently was..." Whitey's voice trailed off. The last time they had all been in the boathouse where the Chris Craft was stored, Hugh had executed the two men who had separately killed his son and granddaughter.

"Right," Tom said.

"I'm thinking it has to be worth something."

Tom felt his throat tighten. Was it sinking in that the old man was really gone from his life? Never to cast his shadow over the bar, the neighborhood and its denizens? He was trying to sort it out in his mind when Whitey interrupted his thoughts.

"I was actually hoping to discuss another matter with you Tommy."

Tom came out of his fog. "What's that?"

Whitey hesitated and then said, "If this isn't the right time?"

"No, it's fine. What is it?"

Whitey opened the top desk drawer and took out a folded sheet of paper and handed it to Tom. He said, "Read this first and then I'll explain."

Tom unfolded the paper and looked at the plain typewritten text:

I know what you did. I know where the bodies are. I have the shovel. I'll be in touch.

That was all it said, no heading or signature. Tom turned the paper over in his hand and looked up at Whitey. "What is this?"

Whitey sighed and sat back in his chair. He rubbed his temples and then said, "I'm going to tell you a story that I only ever told to one person, Hugh. It's about something that I did when I was a kid."

Whitey told Tom about his sudden departure from the Stafford Home for Boys and then added, "Like I said, the only other person I ever told that story to was Hugh, the night he took me in out of the cold. Hell, I never even told my wife or your dad, and we were like brothers."

It suddenly made more sense than ever. Whitey's story was obviously the seed of his fierce devotion to Hugh. Tom whistled and said, "Shit Whitey."

"Shit indeed."

Tom looked at the letter again. "So this is..."

Whitey looked at the piece of paper in Tom's hand and said, "It sounds like the start of someone blackmailing me."

"Is this the only thing you've received?"

"Yes. It came in the mail on Saturday."

Tom thought for a moment. He knew given the circumstances, Whitey wouldn't go to the police. "Do you have the envelope this came in?"

Whitey opened the desk drawer again and removed a white envelope and handed it to Tom. It looked like the same typewriter had been used to address it to Whitey at the bar. It was also postmarked from Niagara Falls two days before. This was one of the times Tom wished he was still a cop. He might have been able to discreetly have it checked for fingerprints. Even that was no guarantee though. It had been handled by other people and machinery along the way.

"This guy, Eddie?" Tom asked.

"Eddie Turner," Whitey said.

"You think he's the one behind this?"

Whitey suddenly looked old and tired, as though the secret he had been keeping had finally worn him down. He nodded and said, "I did something in the heat of the moment, I snapped. I thought Eddie would be on my side, but I guess he didn't want to go down with me. He stayed and faced the consequences while I ran." Whitey looked out the window of the parlor. "I don't know who else it could be."

"And you think that it's not a coincidence that this started after Hugh passed and you took over the business?"

Whitey just nodded.

A number of questions entered Tom's mind, but he knew Whitey probably wouldn't have the answers, not yet anyway. "How can I help you?" he asked.

"I hate to ask you Tom. I know this is my problem..."

"Whitey, don't even say it. You know you're like family to me too."

"Can you find this guy?"

Tom though for a second and then said, "I can try. But what will you do if I find him."

"I just want to talk to him, reason with him."

Suddenly Tom's temples were throbbing. Even with Hugh gone the people in his life had their share of issues. A lot of blood had already been shed within his circle of friends and family.

"I'd ask you to swear to that," Tom finally offered, "but I don't want to put you on the spot. If I do find this guy just let me talk to him first."

Whitey sat back in the chair again and considered what Tom said. "Alright, I've lived with this thing this long. I guess I can accept that."

Chapter 10

Tom had told Whitey he would do what he could, but what would that be? All Whitey had was a name, Eddie Turner, and the fact that he was about the same age as Whitey, early to mid-sixties. Whitey said that he thought Turner was originally from downstate somewhere, White Plains or Yonkers, but he couldn't be sure.

After he got home, Tom booted up his laptop and logged on to a website he used from time to time to look people up through their public records. He had found it fairly useful and purchased a year's subscription for the service. One of these days when he got around to getting organized he knew he would be able to list it as a business expense. It wasn't useful, however, if the person he was looking for had used an alias or a nickname that didn't appear on their public records. If he had the person's real name, former addresses, employment, legal notices and arrest records would all pop up. It amazed Tom sometimes how much about a person's life was floating around the Internet; maybe George

Orwell was right. If he had access to all of this information for $24.98 a year, who knew what someone with more resources could glean?

He started with the most obvious, Edward Turner and got several hundred hits in the State of New York alone. He found only three in the Niagara Falls area, where the cryptic letter had been mailed, but none of them were old enough to have been at Stafford with Whitey in the sixties. He would have to broaden his search geographically and then eliminate them by age. Of course he might not even have the right list of candidates. It might be Edwin or Ned or almost anything else. He got out a legal pad and started making notes.

He was about a half hour into the list and had marked only two possible matches. He was sitting back in the dining room chair rubbing his eyes when his phone buzzed on the table next to his laptop. It was Sherry.

"It's a little early for a beer, but I'll watch you have one," he said instead of a greeting.

"Funny, smart ass," she replied. "Actually I'm at work."

"What's up?"

"Well, Dante is at the D.A.'s office giving a deposition so I'm stuck at the precinct waiting for him. I was catching up on some paperwork when curiosity got the better of me."

Tom had no idea where she was headed but hoped she would get there soon. "Okay," he said.

"Remember last night, when we were talking about Hector Arroyo and Caroline's brother?"

"Yes," Tom said. "As if it were yesterday."

"Again? Well, if you're going to be an asshole."

"Sorry, go on."

"Anyway, remember how absurd we thought the idea was that they might be connected?"

"Yes," Tom said. He really wanted to say he still did.

"I remembered seeing a bulletin last week about this guy, a William Lowery, who got rolled outside the adult bookstore on Clinton. No arrest made and he suffered severe head trauma."

"Still alive?" Tom asked.

"Yeah, but they're saying there might be permanent damage."

Tom sat back and rolled his neck. Then he said, "And, let me guess. Lowery had a history of domestic violence?"

"Yep, two arrests in the last three years. The last one was his mother, with whom he was living while on probation."

"Nice guy..." Tom began.

Sherry picked up when Tom hesitated, "I know what you're going to say Donovan; 'Sherry, you stupid bitch. Three incidents does not a crime wave make.'"

"I would never call you a stupid bitch."

She chuckled and said, "Right. And then I would reply to you that I went back over the bulletins from the last twelve months and looked up assaults without an arrest and cross referenced the victim's names with arrest records and there are a few more than three."

Tom sat up. "How many more than three?" he asked.

"I'm up to six so far. The thing is only three happened in the city and the other three in the 'burbs.'" She paused and then said, "You know how that is, some low life gets his head caved in and..." she trailed off.

"...and it's not a priority," Tom offered.

She didn't say anything for a moment but Tom could hear her breathe. He was wondering if she was still wrestling with her feelings about seeing Arroyo's battered, lifeless body lying in the street.

"Sherry?"

"Yeah... sorry, just thinking."

Tom asked her, "Have you told anyone about this?"

"I wanted to run it by you first. One, because of Caroline's brother, and two, because I know you wouldn't laugh in my face or accuse me of trying to jumpstart my career by going rouge."

Tom smiled and then said, "Why don't you run it by Dante. Maybe this is worth sending up the food chain."

"I don't know..."

Tom had a thought. "I'll tell you what, why don't you send me the list of names? I'll take a look at it and tell you what I think."

"Dante just walked in," she said over the sound of a chair scraping. "We've got to roll... yeah, I'll e-mail the names to you." She sounded hesitant.

"Just the names Sher," Tom said. "If I find anything out it'll stay between us."

"Okay, thanks Donovan," she said as she disconnected.

Tom stood up and went to his front window. This was nuts. Just last night they had shrugged off the idea that somehow there was a connection between Hector Arroyo and Mark Krupp. He wondered if he was just indulging Sherry in her imaginary scenario of someone going around Western New York assaulting people for being wife beaters, child abusers or just assholes in general. He'd learned as a cop and an investigator that there was usually no great conspiracy, no criminal mastermind, just random acts of violence and cruelty. On the other hand, there were a few people or groups of people who were organized and had a plan and the smarts to cover their tracks. He thought about the gangs on the East Side. The most dangerous ones were the ones that kept it on the down low. On the surface they blended in, but everyone in the neighborhood knew who they were. If a message needed to be sent it was sent quickly and without a lot of showmanship. Showing off is what got you noticed by the cops.

He was still wondering what he had gotten himself into with Sherry when he saw Caroline pulling up to the curb behind his car. She was by herself when she got out. Even from his vantage point on the second floor, Tom could see she was upset. He went downstairs and met her in the foyer. Tom looked at her and waited.

Her eyes were red rimmed. She looked at Tom and said, "They're taking Mark off life support."

"What?" Tom asked in spite of himself. When he last talked to Lenny Krupp, he had said that Mark was still hanging on.

"They said the swelling put too much pressure on his brain. Basically it suffocated."

"I'm so sorry Caroline." It was cliché, but it was true. One of those moments in life where you wish you had something profoundly original and comforting, but all that comes out is; "I'm sorry." Tom realized that her son was not with her. "Where's Brandon?"

"With my dad. We're going to stay at his house and go in tomorrow and then..." she teared up again.

Tom reluctantly hugged Caroline. She buried her face into his shirt and he could feel the dampness almost immediately. After a moment she withdrew and looked at his shirt. "Sorry..." she started.

"Don't worry about it," Tom replied. He thought about the questions he had about Mark and his wife Jennifer that he wanted to ask Caroline, but now wasn't the time.

She moved towards her door and said, "I just stopped to grab a few things and head back to my dad's."

Tom was once again at a loss for words. He stepped back and watched her unlock the door and then she turned around and looked at him sadly. "He didn't deserve this." They looked into each other's eyes for a moment and then she turned and went inside.

Shit, Tom thought. The one person who could explain why Mark Krupp was in the park that night was Mark Krupp himself and now he would never have the chance. Tom went back upstairs and back to the window.

What a day. First Whitey and his problems, and now realizing Mark Krupp's legacy would be that of an abusive stalker who got what he deserved. What if there was something to what Sherry was digging into? He had only himself to blame for planting the idea in her head. With his own head now throbbing, he went off to search for the aspirin bottle.

Chapter 11

Donovan was up early the next morning. He made a pot of coffee and was right back in front of his computer. He looked at the legal pad he had been making notes on in his search for Eddie Turner. He was just about to go back to the public record web site when he had a thought and opened his e-mail instead.

There were two messages in his in box, one from Bob Stanley reminding him to send an invoice for the interviews he had done and the other from Sherry Palkowski.

Sherry had sent him an email at 1:30 AM, probably after her shift ended. She had sent him the list of names that she had said were open/unsolved assaults from the past year. Tom opened the attachment and saw that she had included a few details about each case.

As she had said, three were in the city, two apparent muggings and another man jumped outside a bar in the Lovejoy neighborhood. The other three were in the suburbs, one in Lancaster,

one in Tonawanda and the other in West Seneca. All
of the victims had survived their attacks but one,
the man who was stabbed, who died of a heart attack
on his way to the ER. In four of them a blunt object
was used, a club of some type, two of the victims
were stabbed and another was a hit and run. None
of the victims had seen their assailant. Unofficially,
Tom thought, you could add Arroyo's hit and run
and Mark Krupp's beating to those numbers.

He sat back and thought. Assaults and
mayhem occur every day. He wondered if this was a
statistical improbability that all of these men had
records for domestic violence, none of them had
seen their attacker and no witnesses or arrests were
ever made?

Was there a connection? Or was this just his
and Sherry's imagination? He set the hunt for
Eddie Turner aside for the moment and started to
look through the *Buffalo News* online archives for
more on the assaults and the victims.

He wasn't getting too far. After an initial
story in the local section there weren't any follow up
stories on any of the incidents. What Sherry had
said was starting to resonate with him. It was hard
to feel sorry for anyone who took out his
frustrations on women and children. But what
about Mark Krupp? Did he have it coming? Not

according to his family and the less than stellar vibe he got from Mark's wife. He found himself wondering if he was getting carried away with the whole 'avenging angel' scenario. There might be nothing even remotely tying any of this together.

He heard a faint buzz and realized he had left his phone in the kitchen. He walked out and caught it before the fourth buzz. It was his Mother.

"Mom?"

"Hi, Tom. How are you?"

"Fine, mom. How are you?" He could hear the faint sound of traffic in the background.

"Fine. Listen Tom, I know you're busy..."

He had almost forgotten his mother's new boyfriend and the dinner engagement he had missed.

"...but Tony and I are at the Albright Knox and we were wondering if you had a little time this afternoon?"

He didn't want to put it off again so he said, "Yeah, that sounds great."

"We could stop over if you like. We could bring lunch."

Tom looked around his apartment. He couldn't remember the last time he had cleaned it. It wasn't quite a health hazard but then again it wasn't exactly suitable for entertaining. "Um... how about we meet for coffee?" he said.

Tom heard her saying something to Tony and then she came back. "Sounds lovely. Where and when?"

"How about Spot Coffee. It's just down on Elmwood south of Lafayette." He looked at his watch. "Give me thirty minutes?"

"Sounds like a plan, love. See you then."

Good Lord, Tom thought. His mother sounded absolutely giddy. For years after the death of his father and his own legal and personal problems she had been mostly quiet and melancholy. She had been supportive throughout, but Tom knew she was hurting and might have sustained scars to her psyche that would always be there. She had mentioned his Uncle Sam's reservations about Tony Carbone, but how could this be a bad thing? His mother was sixty-three years old; shouldn't she be able to do what made her happy? Of course in Sam's eyes she had a poor track record, marrying the son of a Mick bookmaker from South Buffalo, and look how that had turned out. He dreaded getting involved, but he owed it to his mother.

<<<>>>

Forty minutes later, he'd had trouble finding a parking spot near the coffee shop, he walked in and found his mother sitting at a table with a man of about sixty. When his mother saw him she smiled and stood up. The man did also. He was about six feet tall and had a large frame. His salt and pepper hair was cropped close to his skull and looked to be a little thin on top. He had clear brown eyes and extended a strong calloused hand to Tom.

"Tony Carbone," he said with a smile.

"Tom." And then he said to his mother, "Sorry I'm late. I had to park a couple of blocks away."

She waved it off. "Don't worry about it; although we already ordered." She gestured to a comically large cup in front of her that contained some frothy concoction. He had never known his mother to order anything other than regular coffee. She truly was off the reservation.

"What can I get you?" It was Tony's voice. Tom turned to him and said. "Oh… it's okay I'll just get a coffee."

A few minutes later Tom returned to the table and Rose and Tony were talking quietly gazing into each other's eyes. He cleared his throat and sat down. There was a brief moment of almost awkward silence and then his mother broke it.

"We're you working today, Tom?"

"Nothing serious. Just doing some research from home. I needed a break anyway. How was the museum?"

"We didn't see to much of it," his mother replied.

What did that mean? Tom wondered.

"We went for a string quartet," Tony offered. "My niece is a cellist and I like to listen to her whenever I can."

"She's trying out for the Philharmonic," Rose added enthusiastically.

Another brief lull and then Tom looked at Tony. "Mom said you own a repair shop?"

Tony nodded. "Yeah, had it going on twenty-five years. My son will be taking it over soon."

They made small talk for a while. Tony had been a widower for eight years it turned out. He had a son and a daughter, both in their thirties. The son worked with him, managing the repair shop, his daughter had married an electrician and moved to the suburbs. The daughter had given him two grandchildren; he had the pictures to prove it. He seemed on the surface to be as normal a person as you could find. What was Sam's problem with this guy?

His mother excused herself to go to the ladies room leaving the two men alone. Tom looked into the man's eyes, he looked serene, contented. He didn't know what he was looking for, a tic or a twitch? Some indication that he was actually an axe murderer.

"Mom said you met at St. Margaret's."

Tony smiled ruefully, "Well, we met again at church. We sort of knew each other in a past life."

"Oh?"

Tony looked off in the distance, still smiling. "From the neighborhood." he said. "Back in the day, my dad had a garage on Hertel. Your mom would walk by with her friends every day on her way home from Holy Angels Academy. We had a soda machine out front and one day she was by herself trying to get a soda and the machine ate her money. Well, the old man was out with the wrecker so it was just me in the shop and your mother walks in and sweet as can be tells me she lost her quarter." Tony stopped and shook his head.

"And?" Tom asked.

"And I'd never been more tongue-tied in my life," Tony chuckled. "Here was the prettiest girl in the neighborhood right in front of me and I can't say a word. Your mom said she remembered that but I think she's just being polite. Anyway, after that I made a point to be out front when Holy Angels let out and I would always try to catch her eye and say hello. One smile could make my day."

Good Lord, Tom thought. This guy had been smitten.

"After she graduated from the Academy and I graduated from Bennett, we would see each other at the bars or at the park and she would always say hello. I was saving up my money and I kept telling myself that one of these days I was going to ask Rosalie Dipietro out. Two things stood in my way."

Tom looked over his shoulder towards the rest room. There was no sign of his mother. He looked back at Tony and wondered if he was going to tell him what had kept him from pursuing his high school crush. "What were they?"

"Her brother Sam."

Of course, Tom thought. Even then he was the protective older brother. "Yeah, I could see that," he said.

Tony shook his head. "Rose... your mother tells me you have a complicated relationship with your uncle?" Tony questioned.

"You could say that." Tom wondered where Tony was going.

He shook his head. "Well, back in the day there was nothing too complicated about Sam."

"What do you mean?" Tom asked.

"How do I say this?"

"Say what?"

"Your uncle was kind of a jerk." As he said it, Tony looked at Tom and winced, as if he were expecting Tom to leap up and call him out to defend his family's honor. He was relieved when Tom actually laughed out loud.

"Really?" Tom said.

"Well, he was quick with his fists and he had a bit of a temper. Especially where his sister was concerned. I remember one time this guy was hitting on Rose at the lawn fete and your uncle beat the crap out of him." Tony gestured with his hand, "Not that the guy may have not deserved it, but..."

"It was a little excessive?" Tom finished for him. Tony nodded. "So, you said there were two things. What was the second?

Tony's face fell slightly and he looked down at the table for a moment. He sighed and looked back up at Tom. "I stole a car on my twenty-first birthday."

So that was it, Tom realized. His uncle, one time neighborhood scourge turned career cop, could be stubborn. He had never gotten along with Tom's father and now he probably saw Tony Carbone as another criminal trying to take his sister away. Tom realized he had fallen silent and brought himself back to the conversation.

"Oh... so did they give you probation?"

Tony's face turned from semi-whimsical to totally serious. He said, "That's not the whole story." He paused and looked down at his espresso. "There was this guy on my block, Sal Genusa, and he had this Camaro, all tricked out, T-top, the whole nine yards. The guy was a total peacock, silk shirts, gold chains. My buddy Ralph and me were deep into a twelve pack and we thought it would be funny if we boosted the car and moved it, just to mess with Sal. Well, I hot wired it and we were on our way." As Tony was talking Rose had returned to the table. Instead of stopping, Tony looked at her apologetically and went on. "We were driving down Amherst when Ralph sees a cop car following us. He freaked out because it turns out he has some weed on him and his old man is already on the verge of kicking him out of the house. So I gun it and when I do I ran a red light." Tony closed his eyes and remembered. "We got t-boned by a delivery truck. Ralph died on the spot and I ended up doing two years at Wende Correctional

The table fell silent. Tom noticed his mother put her hand over Tony's. So that was it. Tony's deep dark secret, the thing that made him unsuitable in Sam's eyes. Tom looked at Tony and then Rose. Tony looked truly remorseful, even after almost forty years. His mother looked at Tony and then at Tom. She raised her eyebrows. Tom knew all about remorse. His actions that night in the McKinley Projects had cost him his job, his reputation and almost his freedom. If he didn't believe in redemption, who would?

"That must have been rough," Tom said.

"It was," Tony nodded. "Ralph was my best friend and I was close to his family... well his dad was a piece of work. They never forgave me and I never expected them to."

Silence again as the words settled around them. Tony shook his head and then said, "That was the low point. When I got out, I went back to work for my dad. A year later I met my wife, Lori and we had a pretty good run together. We had the business and two great kids. I realized early on that I couldn't go back and change the past, but I was damned sure I wasn't going to squander the future."

Rose was looking at Tony again, smiling now. It struck Tom to see her so alive and involved again after years of near solitude. How could this be a bad thing? After a moment she changed the subject and they spent another half hour making small talk.

Tom excused himself, got up, kissed his mother and shook Tony's hand.

"It was great to meat you Tom," Tony said earnestly.

"Yeah, same here."

Later that afternoon, Tom was sitting in his flat finishing off a microwave dinner thinking about his mother and her new man. He promised himself that he would call his Uncle Sam and cautiously add his thoughts. He had gone back to his computer and was wondering if he should carry on with Sherry's theory or let that lie. He was sitting staring at the blank screen when his phone buzzed. The caller ID said it was Donovan's

"Tom, it's Whitey."

"What's up?"

Whitey was breathing heavily. "I got another letter."

"What did it say?"

"I just got back to the bar and Bonnie gave me the mail. I took it upstairs to open it... shit!" He was truly agitated.

"What is it?"

"The cock sucker put powder in the envelope. I got it all over my hands when I opened it."

"Jesus Whitey, why aren't you at the ER right now?"

"I opened the letter and it said it was just cornstarch! Do you believe it? He said next time it might be something else."

"Where's the letter now?" Tom asked.

"It's right in front of me on the desk."

"Don't touch it. I'll be right there."

Tom grabbed his jacket and was heading for the door when his phone went off again. He recognized the number as Uncle Sam's landline. Not now, he thought. He let the call go to voicemail and headed for the door.

Chapter 12

Carl Greiner was in a bad way. The bitchy lady at the temp agency had tore him a new one when she found out that the manager at the second-hand store where she had placed him had called her to say that Carl was no longer welcome there. Granted it was a bullshit job anyway, sorting through the garbage people dropped off just to find something the store could sell, but he didn't need the static. All he did was try to ask a girl out.

She reminded him of Lisa. She was small, thin, almost childlike. Like she had better prospects? Lisa. She was the one who had gotten him into a jackpot in the first place.

For three months he had tried to get her attention, tried to get her to understand that he was right for her. She never said she wasn't interested and then all of a sudden the cops were there telling him to leave her alone.

He checked himself in the rearview mirror. He wasn't ugly. Sure, he could probably use a haircut and lose a couple of pounds. Why did they have to be so shallow? He drove down Genesee Street past Best. He had seen the girl before when he was driving around, thinking. She was small too, like Lisa and Kristen, the girl at the thrift shop. This was different, she was a whore.

What a shit hole neighborhood, Carl thought. It was bad enough where he lived, in a crappy apartment off of Doat. He kept looking straight ahead to avoid making contact with the other whores working the street. He didn't need some black bitch leaning into his car and judging him.

There she was, standing with a tall black girl just outside a church of all places. He bumped the curb when he pulled up. The black girl took a quick look around and walked up to the car. She had long toned legs, exposed by the short shorts she was wearing. When she leaned into the car Carl caught a whiff of her sweet perfume.

"Hey," the girl said.

Carl was flustered. He could feel his face getting hot. The sweat was pouring off of him as he just looked at the girl and then tried to look around her at the skinny white girl.

"What's the matter baby? Are you lost?"

Carl shook his head and finally found the words. "Not you, her," he said pointing to the white girl who was lighting a cigarette.

"You don't know what you're missing…" the black girl said in a husky voice.

"Fuck off," Carl sputtered.

The prostitute flipped him off and walked over to the white girl. They started talking, every once in a while glancing over towards Carl. He was getting nervous. He'd paid for sex before but only at the "massage therapy" place in West Seneca. Here he was out in the open, because some two-bit whore reminded him of Lisa. The white girl finished her cigarette and stomped it out. The tall black girl was shaking her head, probably saying something hateful about Carl. She put her hand on the white girl who shook it off and walked over to the car.

Carl got a better look at her inside the car. She was wearing jeans and a worn leather jacket. He tried to guess her age under the make up but couldn't do it. Whatever, she was young and small. Her eyes were tired looking and she had a few acne scars.

"We should go," the girl said. Carl realized he had been frozen, just staring at her. The sweat was beading on his forehead.

"Right," he said and put the car into gear.

"Where…" Carl's voice trailed off. He had no idea where this was going to happen. What had seemed titillating just a short while ago had become nerve wracking.

"See that red brick building up ahead on the right there? Turn down that street and park. It's pretty quiet."

Carl turned his car down Johnson Ave. And pulled up to the curb next to the red brick building which appeared to be some long shuttered business. The rest of the street was a poorly lit collection of houses and vacant lots. He put the car in park and switched off the engine.

He was looking at his hands on the steering wheel when the girl said, "It's twenty for a blow job, fifty for a fuck." She was looking at him impassively.

This wasn't at all what Carl had imagined it would be like. She was rushing him. He looked at her and asked, "How old are you?"

She frowned and said, "Old enough."

Carl looked at her and stared her down. She was nothing at all like Lisa. Still, he was this close to release and went on. "You're not really getting me in the mood."

She blinked her eyes, looked back at him and sighed. "Whatever..."

He was getting angry now. Who was this little bitch to be so dismissive? "I'm fucking serious," he said. "Do you want to earn the money or not?"

Something in his voice made her drop the snotty teenager act. She made an effort to soften her expression. She put a hand on his knee. "Sorry baby, it's just that I'm a little tired."

Carl grunted. "Yeah, well I've had a pretty crappy day myself." Something didn't feel right.

She started to undo his belt. "You're so serious," she said.

Carl looked into her face. She wasn't even trying to hide her apathy or disdain. The red started to creep into the edges of his eyesight. The girl started to unzip his fly. "Do you have the money?" she asked.

"What..." Carl stammered. "Yeah... I got it."

She stopped what she was doing and looked up and half smiled. "Can I have it?"

This was bullshit. Carl was nothing more than a business transaction to her. He shook his head and said, "When you're done."

She hesitated and tried to smile at him again. She put her hand down the front of his pants and then stopped. Something was wrong; Carl wasn't aroused at all, just angry and embarrassed. She looked up into his face and looked both irritated and a little apprehensive. "Do you want to do this or not?" she asked quietly.

"Why, you got some other guys to suck off tonight?"

The girl sat up and glared at him. "Fuck you, dirtbag."

As soon as he heard that Carl brought his right hand up sharply and back-handed her across the cheek. The girl winced and looked at him in stunned silence. He grabbed her by the neck with his right hand, pulled her towards him and then grabbed her by the hair with his left. "Who the fuck do you think you are?" he growled.

Now he was excited, his adrenaline surging. He was back in control. He didn't see the girl slip her right hand into the pocket of the worn leather jacket. He was pondering his next move when he felt the cold air and sting of the box cutter cut into his thigh. His first instinct was to release his hold on the girl and look down at his leg. There was a four-inch gash in his pant leg and the blood was already soaking the entire area. He looked from his leg to the girl who was sitting as far away as she could from him. She looked both terrified and wild, like a cornered animal. He threw a punch at her and she brought her left arm up to block it but it went through and hit the top of her head. She swung the box cutter wildly and nicked his hand as he was about to reload for another blow.

The blood from his hand was now dripping down on the console. His leg was stinging like crazy and he felt a little lightheaded. In the split second he took his attention away from her she had found the door latch and opened it. She tried to roll out of the car but he recovered into time to grab the sleeve of her jacket. She spun back towards him and swung her arm with the cutter but this time he was ready and caught her wrist and turned her arm until she screamed and dropped it. With one last desperate lunge she pushed herself the rest of the way out of the car and rolled to the ground. Carl, who still held onto her right sleeve and left wrist rolled right on top of her. The girl howled. Carl had to shut her up. He was in the process of pinning her down on the cold cement when the back of his head exploded.

First pain and then nothing. He barely felt himself being pushed, no pulled off the girl and rolled over. His eyes lost the ability to focus but he could see a shadow standing above him to his right. It was definitely a man with something in his hand, a tube or a stick. No, it was a club. The shadow raised the club up brought it down quickly. Carl tried to raise his arms but they wouldn't respond in time. Another sharp pain, then red, then nothing.

Chapter 13

Tom made one stop and then drove to the bar and examined the letter. Just to be on the safe side he carefully scooped up some of the powder, placed it in an old pill bottle and told Whitey he would have it tested somewhere. As a further precaution he used the hazardous spill clean-up kit he had stopped and picked up from an E.M.T he knew to give the desk and chair a good going over.

Whitey was still visibly shaken, but now anger was starting to take over. "Bastard," he said. "Scared the crap out of me. After all these years he has to screw with me now!"

Tom examined the envelope, Niagara Falls postmark again. Then the letter. The only thing besides the threat that Whitey had mentioned over the phone was a promise that instructions would soon follow.

Whitey's face was turning from ashen to red. "What's the purpose of this? He already had my attention."

"Although you have to take this seriously, maybe he's just trying to scare you." Tom said as calmly as possible. "He wants you to think he's willing to go that far."

"He has no idea ..." Whitey started. He was glaring at nothing in particular.

"Just give me a couple more days. We need to keep our heads here, Whitey."

"How the hell am I supposed to do that?"

Tom looked him in the eye and said, "Because you have a lot more to lose than he does. Right now he has the upper hand but if we stay calm and do this right we can get the advantage. If it's who we think it is then it's just a matter of time before I track him down and then he loses the only advantage he has."

Whitey was calming down and starting to breath normally. "What about the shovel and the other stuff he said?"

Tom nodded and said, "We find Eddie Turner, we find the shovel too. That's if he even has it."

Now Whitey nodded and looked down, thinking. He looked back up at Tom and said, "Alright... thanks, Tommy."

Tom had gathered his things and was starting for the door to the stairs when Whitey spoke again. "You're never going to believe it," he said.

Tom looked back at Whitey, who was smiling wanly and shaking his head. "Believe what?" he asked.

"You're a lot more like Hugh than you realize."

Tom went home and immediately picked up where he left off with his Internet search for Eddie Turner. After an hour he came up with two finalists who were the right age and shared a downstate place of origin. One, Edward R. Turner, lived in New York City. He'd had trouble with the law in his younger years, mostly small stuff, bad checks, forgery, but for the last twenty or so seemed to have been on the straight and narrow. He was employed, married and owned a home in Queens.

The second, an Edward D. Turner, was much more interesting. He'd been incarcerated half of his adult life, armed robbery, breaking and entering, possessing stolen goods. Unfortunately, his juvenile record was probably sealed; Tom would not be able to tell if Turner had been at Stafford the same time Whitey had been. His last address was listed as an apartment in Albion, NY. There was a state prison in Albion and Tom wondered if Turner had just flopped there after his last stint. This had to be the

Eddie Turner he was looking for. Albion was a lot closer to Niagara Falls than Queens was, and the Albion version hadn't been able to keep his nose clean. Tom looked at his watch. It was after nine PM. He printed out a map to the address in Albion and decided he'd go first thing in the morning.

He heard the front door open downstairs. He stuck his head out and looked down the stairs. Caroline was ushering Brandon in. She looked up and saw him and smiled weakly. Tom could see she had been crying. She opened the door to her flat and told Brandon to go get ready for bed. Tom got to the bottom and waited.

"Mark's gone," she said.

"I'm so sorry Caroline." He truly was this time.

"Thanks," she said looking down.

"Do you need anything?"

"No, we're all set, but thank you. My dad is taking care of the funeral arrangements."

They stood there for a while. Tom wondered if she wanted to ask about his inquiry into Mark's assault. He had nothing new to tell her, just some half-baked idea of his and Sherry's. He took the silence as long as he could and finally said, "Please let me know when the wake and funeral are. And if you need anything at all, a ride, a sitter, anything, just let me know."

She finally looked up at him and with watery eyes she nodded and said, "Thanks." It looked like she wanted to say much more, but was holding back. Tom would have loved to give her the chance so he left it up to her. After a moment she blinked back her tears and went into her flat, leaving Tom out in the hallway.

Back up in his apartment Tom lay awake in bed for a while, feeling helpless. His own words to Sherry were coming back to him about how what you do and don't deserve has nothing to do with what actually happens. That didn't make it any easier though; Caroline and her family didn't deserve any of this. There had to be something he could do to try to achieve some kind of justice.

First though, he had to drive to Albion to track down a blackmailer. Did Whitey deserve what was happening to him? Now there was a gray area. Whitey had started this years ago when he first swung that shovel. Tom knew Whitey was no angel. Still he felt an obligation to Whitey for the loyalty he had shown over the years to himself, his father, and yes, even Hugh.

Chapter 14

The next morning was cool and overcast, good driving weather. Tom left his apartment just before 7:00 AM and just caught the early part of the morning rush on I-90 headed towards the northern suburbs. After that it was clear sailing to Albion.

Albion was a small town that had popped up during the heyday of the Erie Canal. Now it was famous for being the home of two prisons, Albion Correctional, a women's prison, and Orleans Correctional, a medium security men's prison. It looked like a lot of other quaint, small, upstate towns, sort of frozen in time. All the same the shadow of the sprawling prison complex was never far off.

Tom was driving down Main Street at 8:30. He did a slow pass of the address he had for Turner on West State Street. It was a red Victorian style home that had seen better days. He drove down the block, turned around and parked. The house was huge and Tom wondered if it had been divided up into apartments. He took out a small pair of binoculars and looked at the sagging front porch. There was only one mailbox. There was also only one car in the driveway and nothing parked in front on the street. The weeds in the yard were already in full bloom even though it was only mid-June. He put the glasses back in his glove compartment and decided that he had better things to do than stake out this dump all day.

As he approached the front steps a man came out onto the front porch lighting a cigarette. He had long greasy hair and was unshaven. He looked to be in his forties but it was hard to tell. It looked like he'd had a rough life.

"Good morning," Tom said from the bottom of the stairs.

The man looked at him through the cloud of smoke he had just exhaled and said, "Morning."

Tom had found a mug shot of Eddie Turner that was about twenty years old and this guy was too young. He was trying to think of a way to ask about Turner when the man blew out another plume of smoke and asked, "So what are you? Parole? DOC?"

Tom had thought so but now he was sure, the guy had jailbird written all over him. "None of the above," he replied. He decided on the direct approach "Private investigator. I'm looking for Eddie Turner."

The man coughed and spat out something right on the floor of the porch. He looked back at Tom and said, "Never heard of him."

Tom considered the man. There were several possibilities. The address he had for Tuner was wrong and he indeed might not know Turner, he was an accomplice of Turners, or he was just an asshole. He took the picture of Turner out of his jacket pocket and stepped up onto the porch. The man stared at him and then looked at the picture. "Nope, never seen him," he said.

"I have this house listed as his last address," Tom said putting the picture back into his pocket.

"Probably before my time," the man said as he threw the cigarette out onto the weeds. He started to walk past Tom towards the steps. "I've only been here a couple of weeks. You want to talk to Roger."

"Who's Roger?"

"He runs the place. He's probably in the kitchen." With that the man walked down the steps and turned towards Main Street.

Of course, Tom thought, this must be some kind of halfway house. He had double-checked and Turner had served his most recent sentence at

Orleans Penitentiary so this is where he landed when he got out. He walked up to the front door to ring the bell but the button was missing so he knocked. He waited a few minutes in which nothing happened so he knocked again, louder this time. After a moment he heard footsteps and the door swung open and a large black man filled the doorway. He was wearing a white tank top that revealed huge biceps with crude homemade tattoos. He just stared at Tom through the screen door and said nothing.

Tom looked back at him and said, "I need to speak to Roger."

The man put his large hand on the screen door and it swung open slowly. He held it for Tom and shifted his bulk so that there was a small enough opening for Tom to squeeze past into the parlor. All the time the expression on his face hadn't changed. It was a mixture of boredom and distrust.

Tom looked around the parlor. There was an ancient TV in the corner and six folding chairs set up in a circle in the middle of the room. The wallpaper was old and had been peeling for some time. The big man brushed past him and said, "This way."

He followed the man into the kitchen. When his guide tuned aside Tom saw two more men sitting at a small weathered table, a skinny white kid with more bad tattoos and a chubby middle aged guy with graying hair and a neatly trimmed beard wearing jeans and a sweater vest over a white button down shirt. He didn't have to guess which one was Roger.

Roger looked a little startled at first and then stood up and asked, "Can I help you?"

"I was wondering if I could ask you a few questions?" Tom offered.

The skinny kid looked at him nervously. The giant seemed to have disappeared leaving the three of them in the room. Roger looked from Tom to the kid back to Tom. He shook his head and asked, "I'm sorry, but who are you?"

"My name is Tom Donovan, I'm a private investigator." He handed Roger a business card.

Roger frowned at the card and thought for a moment. Finally he looked at the kid and said, "Kyle when you're done put your plate in the dishwasher and start it. It's all ready to go."

The kid just nodded and Roger motioned for Tom to follow him. They went to a room off the kitchen that had probably at one time been a pantry but had been converted into a cramped windowless office. Roger sat down at a small metal desk and

Tom sat in a folding chair that was wedged in next to it. He noticed a picture on the wall. It was a photo of a much younger Roger in priest's attire, being blessed by Pope John Paul II.

"Oh, is it Father Roger?" Tom asked.

Roger shook his head. "Not anymore. It's just Roger now." He was still looking at the business card Tom had given him. He placed it down on the desk and said, "Mr. Donovan, let me be blunt. I am under no obligation to help you with whatever it is you're working on."

"I understand that..."

Roger put a hand up and cut Tom off. "The men living in this house are trying to start a new life for themselves. In order to do that we are trying to get them out of the frame of mind that they are and always will be criminals."

"I appreciate that, but..." Tom started, only to be interrupted again.

"They are not all going to make it on the outside, I understand that." Roger stared hard at Tom. "For the ones who are making an effort, I can't have the public coming in here stirring things up whenever they feel the need."

Tom waited to make sure Roger was done this time. "I'm sorry to have just shown up here without calling but given the sensitive nature of what I'm doing..." he hesitated.

"What are you doing, Mr. Donovan?"

"It's very important that I talk to a man named Eddie Turner."

Roger sat back and sighed. "Eddie Turner," he said.

"Does Eddie live here?"

Roger was thinking of something and then he came back around and looked at Tom. "He did."

Shit, Tom thought. "He did?"

"He moved out six months ago. What did he do?"

Something about Roger's tone of voice and the way he phrased the question told Tom that he was on the right path. Roger had dropped all pretense of private rehabilitation and simply asked what Turner was up to now. Tom had crossed paths with more than a few ex-convicts when he was a cop. He knew the recidivism rate was high and was more than a little jaded on the concept of rehabilitation. Sometimes he had wondered if a stretch in prison made people worse.

"All I can say is he may be involved in an extortion scheme," Tom said.

Roger fell silent and stared at his desk. Tom interrupted his thoughts, "You're not surprised?"

"Not entirely, no," Roger said. "Eddie Turner was one of the few men who I thought was too far gone."

"What do you mean?"

"A career criminal who had basically wrecked his body and his mind, even his soul, with alcohol and drugs." Roger stopped and looked back up at Tom. "Who is he allegedly blackmailing?"

"I have a client back in Buffalo."

"Why don't they call the police?"

Tom had told Roger as much as he was going to, especially considering the fact that Turner was no longer a resident. "All I can say is it's a very sensitive issue. My client is hoping we can locate Mr. Turner and try to reason with him. Failing that, we will go to the authorities." Roger sat back and crossed his arms. Tom wondered what he was thinking and didn't want to seem like he was being aloof or shady. He needed one more piece of information from Roger and he didn't want him to shut down. "My client is a legitimate businessman in Buffalo. Unfortunately, when he was a teenager he got into trouble and he crossed paths with Turner at the Stafford Home for Boys. We think Turner is threatening my client with revealing some embarrassing information from their time together at Stafford that my client would rather forget."

Roger narrowed his eyes and waited. Tom decided to appeal to his ideal that men could be rehabilitated. "My client hasn't been in trouble with the law since he left Stafford." This was technically true, although shaded in gray. "Now Turner is threatening him with dragging out all of this history. Things that even my client's family doesn't know about."

Roger looked like he was going to ask something and then seemed to realize that was all the information he was going to get. He uncrossed his arms and sat back in his chair. "Well, like I said, I'm not entirely surprised that Eddie may have been involved in something like this but..." he paused.

"But?"

"Eddie Turner moved out six months ago. It wasn't that we had given up on him entirely but he was sick, too sick to take care of himself."

"Sick? What did he have?"

Roger replied, "A lot of things. The short answer would be that he was a victim of a misspent life. The drugs and the alcohol and the blackness of his soul wore him down."

Roger paused and scratched the bridge of his nose, then continued, "And that's the thing. There's not much of Eddie left."

"What do you mean?"

"Even if he was willing to go into blackmailing people, I don't think he has the faculties."

"I'd still like to speak to him, even if it's only to clear him and move on. Where is he now?"

Roger thought for a moment and then nodded. "We tried to place him in a nursing home here in Albion but couldn't find one that would take him. The county home is overflowing and the private ones were out of the question. Eddie is indigent. We eventually found a bed for him at the Niagara County home in Lockport."

Tom thanked Roger and apologized again for the intrusion. If Eddie Turner was still in Lockport that put him that much closer to Niagara Falls, the source of Whitey's blackmail letters. But what if what Roger said was true, that Turner had made such a mess of himself that he could barely function, let alone mastermind an extortion scheme. There was only one way to find out. Tom put the address of the Niagara County Home into his phone and headed west towards Lockport.

Chapter 15

It was a straight shot eastbound on Rt. 31 from Albion to Lockport and Tom covered it in just over a half hour. The County Home was located on the Eastern edge of the city on Davison Road. It was a two-story block style building without much curb appeal. Tom found his way to the main entrance and walked up to a bored looking security guard at the front desk.

"Can I help you?" the guard asked.

"I'm here to visit my uncle, Edward Turner."

The guard shot him an odd look and then finger pecked a few keys into an old coffee stained keyboard on the desk. He looked over the rims of his glasses at the monitor. He grunted as he handed a clipboard to Tom to have him sign in and then said, "Room 207." He jerked his thumb over his shoulder and then added, "Through those doors, the elevator will be to your right." Tom turned to leave and the guard said, "Hey, you need this." And he handed Tom a worn, laminated visitor's pass.

Tom took the dingy elevator up to the second floor. As soon as he rounded the corner into the main hallway it hit him—the smell of disinfectant trying to mask the odor of human waste and sickness. There was no nurses' station per se, like you would find in a hospital so Tom just made his way to room 207.

The door was open and he stepped quietly into the room. The TV was blaring a game show at top volume. There were two beds in the room and they were both occupied. In the bed nearest the door was an older black man with slack skin and rheumy eyes. He glanced at Tom and said, "Got a smoke?"

"No, sorry."

"The fuck good are ya'?" the man said and turned his attention back to the screen.

There was a partition blocking Tom's view of the other bed so he entered deeper in the room and when he reached the foot of the bed he found Eddie Turner, or at least who he thought was Eddie Turner. The man in the bed had aged poorly and Tom had to take out his picture of Turner from twenty years ago to make sure. He had lost about twenty pounds and most of his hair. His gray skin hung loosely off of his face. He was asleep or possibly dead, Tom thought, he stared at Turner to make sure his chest was rising and falling.

"You his kin?" the man in the other bed asked Tom. Tom looked over at the man and only then noticed that there was only the outline of one leg under the covers.

"No, just a friend," he replied.

Tom was wondering if Turner was playing possum, especially when a stranger was standing at the foot of his bed. He looked at Turner's roommate and asked, "How long have you been in this room with him?"

"Couple of months." He shook his head. "Mother sleeps twenty-three hours a day, barely eats. 'Course the food in here is so bad can't say I blame him." He looked at Tom again. "Sure you don't have a ciggy?"

"Sorry."

Tom looked back at Turner and considered his options. He could wait for him to wake up and question him or he could try to gently prod him back into the world of the living. Unless his roommate was lying for him and was part of the conspiracy he was starting to wonder if Turner had the wherewithal to run a blackmail scheme, not without help anyway. He had a thought and stepped over to the roommate. The man eyed him suspiciously. "I could get you a pack of smokes," Tom said as quietly as possible given the TV's volume.

The man knew what was what, "What I got to do?" he asked.

"Answer a couple of questions, that's all."

"Like what... are you a cop?" he asked distrustfully.

"Nope."

"You get the smokes and then I'll tell you my life story."

Tom was getting impatient. "That's not how it works, I'm in a hurry." He took a twenty-dollar bill out of his wallet and held it up. "You can use this to bribe one of the orderlies for cigarettes or whatever you want to do with it, but I need to ask you about Eddie," he jerked his thumb over his shoulder towards Turner.

The old man looked hard at the twenty and then nodded, "Go ahead," he said.

Tom's head felt like it was about to split open. He grabbed the remote for the TV and muted it. "Does Eddie have any regular visitors?"

"Nope, ain't seen a soul come in here to see him."

There were two phone jacks in the wall between the two beds but Tom didn't see a phone. He asked anyway, "What about phone calls?"

"Phone cost money." The man said. "Don't think Eddie won the Sweepstakes or anything."

Tom could hear footsteps coming down the hall. He handed the bill to the man and said, "You better stash this," and then asked, "What about the staff here? Does he talk to any of them?"

The old man shook his head and said, "Never heard him say nothin' to nobody. Course I don't watch him 24-7."

"What do you mean?"

"Well they take us out sometimes. If the weathers nice, or if they is a movie or somethin' in the common room..." he stopped and looked towards the door.

Tom turned and saw a tall woman with blond hair turning white standing in the doorway glaring at him. She was wearing an olive green jacket and a long skirt. Behind her was the security guard who had signed him in who looked a little red in the face. There was something familiar about the woman that Tom couldn't put his finger on.

After a momentary silence Tom said, "Hello."

Tom's new friend said, "Shit, it's nurse Ratched."

The woman shot him a withering look and then turned back to Tom. "What do you think you're doing?" she asked.

"I'm here to see Eddie Turner." He pointed to the partition behind which he was pretty sure Eddie was still just lying there.

"What business do you have with Mr. Turner?"

Tom's initial impulse was to tell her that whatever it was, it was none of her goddamned business but he fought it off and said, "We have a mutual friend."

She shook her head and frowned. "Mr. Turner isn't allowed to have visitors."

Tom had never heard of a nursing home restricting access to its residents. As far as he knew, Turner had served his time and was a free man. He was thinking of a non-confrontational way to protest but she went on.

"You're going to have to leave. James will escort you to the lobby." She stepped aside and James the security guard took a step forward. He wore an expression of both irritation and embarrassment. He held up his hand and beckoned Tom forward. Tom looked at the man on the bed. The twenty dollar bill was nowhere in sight. As he walked by the woman in charge he smiled at her. Damned if he hadn't seen her before. He and James rode the elevator down in silence.

When they reached the lobby Tom asked, "Who's the lady?"

James looked at him sourly and after a moment said, "That's Peggy. She's the administrator."

"She seems nice."

James looked at him, confused at first but then he caught the sarcasm. It did nothing to brighten his mood. They had reached the entrance and he gestured with his hand for Tom to keep going.

Tom thought about Turner as he made his way south on Transit Road back towards Buffalo. At first blush, and after what his roommate said, Eddie Turner was more dead that alive. How the hell could he be behind a blackmail? But at the same, time who else could it be? Whitey had claimed that only himself, Turner and Hugh knew the truth about what happened at Stafford. Of course Turner could have told anyone willing to listen about the crazy kid he was in reform school who killed a guard and went over the wall. Still, it had to be someone who had put it all together and made the connection between Francis Czerny the juvenile delinquent and Whitey Brennan the bar owner. If Turner wasn't involved it was someone that he knew or had crossed paths with.

He felt his phone vibrate and took it out of his pocket. It was Sherry's cell phone.

"What's up?" Tom asked.

"You know the crazy-assed theory we hatched about a serial vigilante?" she asked.

"Yeah?"

"I think we have another body."

Chapter 16

Sherry didn't have time to talk so they agreed to meet at Cole's on Elmwood after her shift ended. Tom got back on the road and made his way back towards the city.

It was going on four o'clock when he made it to the tavern. Whitey seemed anxious and ushered Tom upstairs to the office. He didn't take time out for pleasantries. He closed the door behind them and asked, "You found him?"

"Yeah," Tom replied. "Only Eddie isn't doing too well, as far as I could tell."

Whitey was flustered. Obviously he thought his problem would go away with a warning to Turner. "What do you mean?"

"The guy appears to be half dead Whitey." Tom replied. "He didn't look like he could seal an envelope let alone mount a blackmail scam."

Whitey pondered that for a moment. "How bad is he?" he finally asked.

"Well, I'm not a doctor, but between what I saw and what his bunkmate said, I don't think he's sandbagging anyone."

"Fuck," Whitey said. Tom had very seldom heard Whitey curse. He shook his head and added. "Who else could it be?"

"It was a long time ago Whitey. Turner has been in and out of prison for most of his life. He could have told anyone."

"But..." another head shake "...who could make the connection?"

"What connection?" Tom asked.

"I've been living under a different name all these years. As far as anyone knows Francis Czerny vanished in 1967."

Now Tom stopped to think. The chance that some low life Turner had met figured all this out was probably remote. "There was one thing that was kind of odd." he said.

Whitey seemed lost in thought. It took a moment for what Tom said to register. "What's that?" he finally asked.

"I got the bum's rush at the County Home. Escorted off the premises and everything. The more I think about it the more off it seems."

"So what do we do now?"

"It might be worth it if I take a look at the home. See who's who?"

Whitey pulled a face. Clearly he wanted to put this behind him. Tom assured him that he would keep at it until they figured out who was pulling the strings. Tom left knowing that Whitey was not the least bit appeased.

Back at his apartment, Tom searched the Internet for information on the Niagara County Home with little success. There was a brief blurb about it on the county's web site with some contact information, but there was no listing of current staff members. He tried digging further into Turner's past but nothing jumped out at him and the trail ended at the halfway house in Albion.

After he ate, he made a call he wasn't looking forward to but knew he had to do it. He went down the front stairs and knocked on Caroline's door. He could hear the TV, it sounded like an MMA fight, and after a moment Caroline opened the door, wearing jeans and a sweater. She looked tired. She stepped out into the hallway and partially closed the door behind her.

"How are you?" Tom asked.

She smiled slightly and said, "I'm okay I guess."

"And Brandon?"

She looked over her shoulder at the door. "It's hard to say. This is one of those times that I wish I knew what was going on in that head of his." Tom thought he saw her fighting back the tears again.

Once again he found himself failing to come up with something to say. The silence was starting to get to him when Caroline recovered and said, "The wake is tomorrow at Rogers and Sons in Kenmore. The funeral is Friday at St. Luke's."

"I'll be there," was all that came out.

She looked at him and smiled. She seemed to be thinking of something. "We still haven't heard anything from the police," she said.

Tom had nothing new to tell her either. He had let Whitey's situation sidetrack him. He knew better than to make another promise that he couldn't keep. At the same time, he resolved that he would not let Mark Krupp die a statistic. "I don't want to get your hopes up..."

She shook her head. "You've already done more than I could ask. My dad and I appreciate it."

Her words did little to assuage the feeling that he hadn't done anything. They said good night and Tom went back upstairs. The first thing he was going to do was talk to Sherry about the latest victim. He had been on the go since early in the morning so he stretched out on his bed and closed his eyes before heading off to meet her at Cole's.

He woke up at 10:30, groggy and with a bad taste in his mouth. It was starting to dawn on him that his body was starting to protest if he didn't get enough sleep. In the old days he could go for days on a few hours here and there.

He got to Cole's at 11:15 and did a quick scan of the dimly lit bar area, but there was no sign of Sherry. He figured she was probably on her way from the station on Esser Avenue or maybe she had a last minute report to file. He grabbed a seat at the bar and ordered a beer. There were only a few other customers at the bar, mostly in groups of twos and threes. Tom absent-mindedly turned his attention to the baseball game on the TV over the bar.

Twenty-five minutes later and still no Sherry. Tom tried her cell phone but it went to her voicemail. He was still tired and the beer wasn't helping. He would give it a few more minutes and then he would go. He was in the process of scooping up his change and leaving a tip for the bartender when she finally came in.

She was wearing jeans and a leather jacket. Two guys in their early twenties by the door gaped at her as she walked up to where Tom was sitting.

She nodded. "Agreed."

"Let me make a couple of calls and see if we can figure out where this guy is coming from."

Sherry looked down with her brow furrowed. Whoever this guy was, he'd rattled her.

"In the mean time," Tom said, "you said that we might have another one.

Sherry broke out of her momentary trance and replied, "Yeah... right... some lowlife named Carl Greiner got his head caved in the other night. It looked a lot like a couple of the other ones except he was cut up too. Something sharp like a razor."

"Where was this?" Tom asked.

"Off of Genesee. They think he branched out from being a first rate stalker to soliciting and got rolled for his troubles."

"Stalking?" Tom asked.

"Yeah, Greiner had a history of pursuing women who had no interest in him whatsoever. Scared the shit out of the last girl. Bad enough for her to move out of town."

"Witnesses?"

"Not at the scene. He was found outside his car and both doors were open. The theory is he got jumped while he was in a compromising position."

Guess again, Tom thought to himself. When he looked at her he noticed she looked worried.

"What's up?" he asked.

She looked at him and then around the bar and then back at him. "I don't really feel like a beer," she said. "Can we get out of here?"

This didn't sound good, Tom thought to himself. As they walked towards the exit he noticed the same two young men looking at him with apparent envy. Wrong again, he thought.

Out on the street she seemed agitated and nervous. He had a brief thought that maybe he had been wrong about her, maybe she wasn't cut out to be a cop. Was the job getting to her already?

They walked down Elmwood. The night had cooled considerably and it helped sharpen Tom's focus. "Sherry, what's going on?"

She stopped in front of a darkened florist's shop and looked around again. "That body I told you about..." she started.

"Yeah?"

"We got back to the station a little before eleven and I was back on the computer looking at the report on the victim and I got a call."

"From who?"

"Some guy at Central Police Services. He saw my log in ID and asked me what I was looking for."

CPS was an agency run by Erie County to provide support and comunication between the various law enforcement entities in the area. It was mostly administrative but they also coordinated 911 calls and provided forensic assistance and training to whoever needed it. It made sense that Sherry's inquiries might be noticed after awhile; the crimes were spread out across several jurisdictions.

"What did you tell him?" Tom asked.

"As little as possible. I made up some crap about knowing the victim."

"Did he buy that?"

"Nope. He asked me about one of the other reports I was looking into and I ran out of bullshit to hand him so I said I was just curious." She stopped and grimaced. "Then he gave me a warning."

"What did he say?" Tom asked.

"He said since I was still a probationary I should kick any knowledge I had up the chain to the detectives at the precinct or to CPS if it's multiple jurisdictions. He made it sound like I was hiding something."

"Did he tell you his name?"

Sherry shook her head. "He said it really fast when I picked up, Franks or French or something. I wish I would have been paying better attention because I sure as hell wasn't going to ask him to repeat it," she said.

"No, I get that." Tom paused and had a thought. "Did the brass at the precinct say anything about it?"

She looked at him. "No. Not yet, but there's always tomorrow."

Tom looked off down Elmwood. "Something about this is a little off."

"What do you mean?"

He faced her again. "Any dealings I ever had with CPS were never that direct. If they had a beef with somebody they would call your commander or somebody downtown. It's a little weird that he would call you directly and even weirder that he would call you at eleven o'clock at night."

She looked at him hopefully at first, but a cloud seemed to cross over her. "So what do you mean?" she asked.

"I don't know yet, but I think you should down on the research for awhile, at least to figure out who this guy is and how much he's willing to make. The last thing you want is to screw up your probation."

171

"Alright," Tom said. "You cool it on the research for awhile. I've got a couple of things I can check on."

Chapter 17

The next morning Tom made a call he wasn't comfortable making, but it was a place to start.

"Tom?" his uncle Sam said when he picked up his phone.

"Hey, Sam."

"I've been wondering when you'd pop up."

"Oh, Why is that?" Tom asked.

There was a pause and then Sam said, "I hear you met your mother's new friend."

Shit, Tom thought. He really didn't want to get into his mother's love life right now. The reason for his call was already delicate enough. "Yeah, we had coffee."

Another awkward silence followed. Tom got tired of waiting and decided to get the unpleasantness over with. "He seems like a nice guy."

Sam snorted and said, "I'm sure he's a real charmer."

"Mom mentioned that you're not crazy about the whole thing."

"That's one way to say it."

Tom was getting frustrated but he didn't want to upset his uncle. He decided to play the analyst. "What's this all about Sam?" he asked.

"What do you mean? 'What's this all about?'"

"This animosity towards Tony."

Sam seemed to be holding his breath, and Tom sensed he was grimacing. "The guy's a Jailbird, Tom," Sam blurted out. "A convicted felon."

Tom lowered his voice, not wanting to sound confrontational. "Sam, that was a lifetime ago."

It didn't work. Sam raised his voice. "Are you kidding me? Maybe you don't know your mother as well as I do then."

"What does that mean," Tom said suddenly feeling defensive.

"Her taste in men," Sam sputtered. "It's always been for shit!"

Now Tom was angry. "So, this is still about Dad?"

"No Tom it's not. Your mother and I came to peace with that a long time ago. You know that!" Sam paused as if trying to calm himself down. "I've always been a little overprotective of your mother. She was always too nice, and there was always some wolf sniffing around."

Tom was doubtful that it had nothing to do with Rosalie Dipietro marrying the rough- neck son of a South Buffalo bookie. But Sam had been good to them after his father was murdered and he tried to keep that in mind. "Uncle Sam," he said, "this guy Tony isn't my dad, and mom's not some naive teenager anymore. And I've got to tell you, I haven't seen her this happy in a long time."

He could hear Sam breathing on the other end and knew that Sam had made his argument and was going to stick to it, at least for the time being. "Just think about it, okay?" Tom added.

"I don't know," Sam said.

Tom seized the lull to get down to what the real purpose of his call was. "Do you know anybody who works at CPS?"

"Why?" Sam asked after a moment. Tom wondered if he should even press on considering his uncle's mood. He knew he had to phrase his inquiry carefully.

"You know Sherry Palkowski? The girl I used to work with at the agency?"

"Yeah," Sam replied. "I hear good things about her from her division CO."

Well that was good at least, Tom thought. "Well she got an odd call from a guy at CPS and it kind of spooked her."

There was another pause and then Sam said, "Why would you be getting involved?"

"I'm not really–"

Sam cut him off. "I know she's your friend Tom, but this should go through proper channels."

"She didn't want to make any waves," Tom offered.

"I understand that. But if somebody is harassing her there is a procedure in place to handle it. And I don't mean sweep it under the rug. The department is very sensitive to that kind of thing and they don't take a shine to outsiders sniping at them."

That was it, Tom knew. He had been a cop for ten years and now he was an "outsider." If his uncle was anything it was by the book, whether you were family or not. Sam was probably the biggest reason Tom was able to get on at the BPD, but after that Tom was treated just like every other recruit, maybe even judged more acutely. He had to back peddle. "I just thought I'd ask," he said trying to mask his disappointment. "I understand what you're saying."

"Good," Sam said. "Look, I've got to go, but why don't you come over for dinner sometime this week? Your Aunt Dianne would love to see you and we can talk about this Tony situation over a glass of wine."

"Sounds good." They said goodbye and Tom disconnected.

This was going to be harder than he thought. When he was with Frederickson and Associates he could always go to Brian Dinkle, the agency's IT man, to do a little cyber sleuthing. That all ended when Dinkle drew the wrath of the Federal Government and went underground. Tom thought about anyone else he knew and the first name that popped into his head was Rod Barlow, the security consultant that he freelanced for.

Rod Barlow, in addition to running his own security firm, was also registered as a New York State Peace Officer and had contacts all over. He had consulted for the Seneca Indians on casino security and surveillance and ran a class for security guard certification. Tom remembered him saying he had dealings with Central Police Services as well. He decided to drive down to Barlow's office on Seneca Street and then he would go on to Mark Krupp's wake.

Barlow kept an address in an old machine shop that had been shuttered and then re-purposed as office space. Barlow liked it because it was just South of downtown and it had a fenced in lot, video surveillance as well as plenty of storage space for the tools of his trade. Tom knew Barlow didn't spend all that much time in his office but he took the chance, knowing he would probably do better face-to-face than over the phone.

He was in luck. Barlow buzzed him in the front entrance after he rang the bell. Tom entered the office on the right side and found Barlow standing by a file cabinet.

"Mr. Donovan," Barlow said cheerfully, as he finished filing some papers. "What brings you here on this fine morning? Do I owe you money too?"

"No," Tom smiled back at him. "I was wondering if you could help me out with something."

Barlow eyed him with feigned suspicion. He turned and walked back to his desk with a limp he had acquired when he blew out his knee playing basketball for St. Bonaventure in the seventies. Barlow stood about six foot four and wore a full beard. He looked more like a college professor than a cop. "Sounds pretty serious," he said. "And that sharp suit adds to your gravitas."

Tom looked down at the only suit he owned and shook his head. "I'm on my way to a wake."

Barlow sat down behind his desk and motioned Tom to a chair. "Sorry to hear that," he said. "What can I do for you?"

Rod Barlow was not someone you could bullshit or manipulate so Tom told him the whole story, Mark Krupp, the other assaults and Sherry. Barlow listened without interruption until Tom finished with the question, "I was wondering if you knew anybody who works at Central Police Services?"

Barlow picked up a pen and wrote something down on the legal pad in front of him. He looked up at Tom and said," This sounds pretty serious. Has your friend considered running this up the chain of command?"

"That's just it. She was just doing a little digging around when she got this cryptic call from the guy at CPS."

"And?" Barlow raised his eyebrows.

"And we just want to know who this guy is. That's all."

Barlow stood up and picked up the pad. "As it turns out," he said, "I do know a few people at CPS. I can make a discreet inquiry into this . . ." he looked at the pad, "Franks or French and get back to you."

Tom stood up and shook Barlow's hand. "Thanks Rod," he said. "And come to think of it, did you mail out my check for the thing in Albany?"

Barlow smiled and shook his head. "I did yesterday, you goddamned mercenary."

Chapter 18

Tom made it to Rogers and Sons Funeral Parlor at 4:10 PM. The room was fairly full. Judging by the look and age of the crowd it seemed the majority were family or contemporaries of Mark's father Lenny. Caroline spotted Tom and came over to give him a hug. She introduced him to a few of her friends and cousins and then Tom spotted Brandon. He was sitting in a wing-backed chair in the corner looking miserable. He was staring down into his lap scowling. There was a wide circle around his resting spot as if no one wanted to be near him. Tom leaned over to Caroline and when he was sure no one else was listening he said, "Would you mind if I took Brandon across the street for ice cream?"

Caroline looked at Tom and then at Brandon and sighed. She looked back at Tom and smiled and said, "That would be great."

Brandon was more than agreeable to leave the wake for a while. His face relaxed as soon as they were out of the room. They crossed the street without saying anything and ordered two small vanilla cones.

"Pretty tough day, huh?" Tom said after they found a bench in the sun. Brandon said nothing at first, he just ate his ice cream. Tom was beginning to understand what Caroline meant when she said she wished she knew what was going on in his head.

Brandon stopped eating for a moment and said, "I liked Uncle Mark, he made me laugh."

"Sounds like he was a nice guy."

Brandon looked across the street at the funeral home. "All those people in there. I don't know them."

Tom thought he might know where Brandon was going. "I don't like these things either," he said. "This is one of those things people do to say goodbye to someone. Just because you and I don't like it, it's still important to your mom and your granddad."

Brandon had refocused his attention on his ice cream, which had started to run down onto his hand. "I know," he said. "I just get nervous around strangers."

"You should come upstairs and work on the bag again sometime."

Brandon's face clouded over briefly and Tom was afraid he'd said something wrong. "I'm sorry, I thought you liked it."

"I did," Brandon said. "But my hands hurt after..."

"That happens," Tom said, relieved. "I think I have an old pair of gloves you can use next time. We'll see how that works."

They finished up and went back across the street. Tom made sure Brandon found the men's room to wash his hands and then returned him to his mother. He was still quiet but his mood had definitely improved. Tom scanned the room thoroughly for the first time. Not that he was surprised, but Mark's widow, Jennifer, was nowhere to be seen.

He was making his way over to Lenny Krupp to offer his condolences when his phone vibrated. He slipped into the hallway and answered it.

"I got another package in the mail," Whitey said.

"Did you open it?"

"Not yet."

"I'm on my way," Tom said disconnecting the call.

Whitey looked ashen when Tom walked into his office over the tavern. He was sitting at his desk looking at a small padded envelope like it might go off at any second. Tom retrieved the hazardous spill kit from the corner and said, "Let's take this out back."

Out behind the building Tom donned the gloves and respirator from the kit and Whitey filled a bucket with water and was standing by. Tom carefully tore off the edge of the envelope and dumped it out onto the ground. There was a cell phone with a piece of paper wrapped around it. Tom checked the envelope but there was nothing else in it. He opened up the paper and there was a typewritten note on it:

Answer this at 8:00 tonight.

He peeled off the gloves and the respirator and held the phone up to Whitey. "Well, here's their next move," he said.

"A phone?"

"Pre-paid, probably. I'm guessing with cash and a sister phone to be used and discarded after they're done with you."

"Son of a bitch," Whitey fumed. "What the fuck do they want?"

"We're going to find out at eight I guess."

Tom took notice that he had perspired right through his shirt. It was just after six and he thought he had better get home and get changed and then he could come back and wait for the call. He had just gotten in when Rod Barlow called him.

"Thomas, I think I have something for you," Barlow said.

"Jesus, that was fast."

"Well, it's second hand info, friend of a friend kind of thing. But I think it might be something."

"What is it?"

"I'm going to e-mail it to you. But it's going to cost you." Tom could picture a smile playing across Barlow's face.

"And what would that be, Rod?"

"You know the concert at the arena this Saturday?"

"No."

"Oh yeah, big hip-hop show. Lots of bling and gangsta stuff. I need a couple of people backstage."

"I'll do it," Tom said quickly. He wasn't crazy about the idea but it was work and he couldn't say no to Rod, especially if he had come through for him.

"You're a prince Tom. Check your inbox and meet us at the office at 5:00 PM on Saturday."

"Thanks Rod..." Tom started but Barlow was already gone.

He booted up his laptop and opened his email. There were two messages from Bob Stanley. Tom silently cursed to himself. He had gotten so involved with Whitey and Mark Krupp that he hadn't answered his mail in several days. Despite the fact that he had bills to pay however he opened the message from Barlow first. There was a file attached that Tom downloaded and opened.

It looked like at least part of a personnel file for a man named Phillip Benzinger, an employee of CPS. The file said that Benzinger had retired from the Erie County Sheriff's Department in 2012. He was only forty-five at the time of his retirement and when Tom scrolled down he found out why. There was another part of the attachment that stated that Benzinger had been placed on administrative leave towards the end of his career as a Sheriff's Deputy for pointing his service weapon at his daughter's boyfriend and threatening him in front of multiple witnesses. No charges were pressed and six months later Benzinger was with CPS, listed as a community liaison and firearms instructor. There was a picture of Benzinger in his deputy's uniform. He looked serious, almost angry. Barlow had added his own note saying that Benzinger had been at CPS teaching a class on the night that Sherry got the call.

Tom checked his watch; it was after seven. He wanted to make sure he was back at Donovan's before eight to be with Whitey when he got the call but his curiosity was killing him. He had no idea how many people Barlow's source had vetted before they came up with Benzinger. And the incident with the boyfriend. What was the story behind that? Was it an abusive relationship that Benzinger decided to put a stop to, a move that jeopardized his career? Or was he just some overprotective hot head? Either way, the fact that he was a firearms instructor told Tom that Benzinger liked his guns and should be tread carefully around.

He went into his bedroom and got his own gun out of the safe he had bolted to the floor in his closet. Better safe than sorry, he thought. He pulled a jacket on and was headed to the door when his phone buzzed again. It was Whitey.

"No need to come tonight lad," Whitey said. He sounded exhausted.

"What do you mean?"

"They called already."

Shit, Tom thought. "What did they say?"

"They want twenty-five grand by tomorrow night or they go to the state police."

"Did the voice sound familiar? Like Turner or somebody else you've crossed paths with?"

"No," Whitey said. "They were using one of those things that changes your voice. And yes," he said preemptively, " the caller ID was blocked."

Tom's mind was racing but then he told himself they had at least a day to figure out what to do. "Can you get your hands on that kind of cash?" he finally asked.

"I can... I guess..."

"If anything Whitey, just to buy us time. You know once they have their hooks into you they'll bleed you dry."

Whitey sighed and said," I know."

"Let's make it look good. You and I will talk tomorrow and we'll figure something out. The fact that they called early tells me they are just as anxious as you are. I think we may be dealing with a novice." Tom wasn't sure if he believed that himself but he had to keep Whitey on point until they could figure out what to do. Whitey was silent so Tom came back and said, "I know this is going to sound stupid, but try and get some rest tonight. We're going to need to be sharp tomorrow."

Whitey mumbled something and they ended the call. There was nothing else he could do for Whitey tonight. Tom was still pumping adrenaline though and knew a quiet night at home was out of the question. He looked at his laptop. The picture of

Phillip Benzinger looked right at him. If he couldn't do anything for Whitey tonight, maybe he could do something for the Krupps.

Chapter 19

10:45 PM and Donovan was driving west
down Genesee Street. He was dressed urban-casual,
hooded sweatshirt and a ball cap pulled low over his
eyes. He had debated with himself about what to
wear, on the one hand he didn't want to look like a
john, but on the other hand he didn't want to look
like a cop. The people he was looking for spooked
easily.

The last couple of years he had been a cop he
mostly worked on the gang task force. He had little
interaction with the girls on the stroll but he'd
known who they were and where they worked. He
wondered how many of the girls he knew were still
around. It had been almost five years since he
worked this neighborhood and the shelf life of a
prostitute around here was pretty short. Drugs,
violence and other health problems took their toll.

He spotted a few girls clustered together and
when he slowed slightly they shot him a few fleeting
glances. He pulled to a stop and one of the older
girls looked around and then came over.

The passenger side window in his Chevy rolled down reluctantly and then the woman bent over and looked in. Her hair was braided tightly on her head and the skin on her face was drawn sharply on her cheekbones. She looked more like an Amazon warrior than a paramour.

"You need something mister?" she asked.

"I'm looking for a friend," Tom said.

"Then you in the wrong fucking neighborhood." She glared at him and shook her head.

Tom turned over his hand and showed her a twenty. "I just need to ask you a question and then you can get on with whatever it is you're doing."

"The fuck?" she said. She looked at Tom and then at the twenty. "You police?"

"Nope... one question, that's all. " He held out the twenty. The woman reached for it, but he pulled it back slightly.

She hissed at him and he thought she was going to walk away. She must have changed her mind; this would be the easiest twenty she earned all night. "What's the question then?" she asked.

Tom unfolded a piece of paper and showed it to her. There was a picture of Carl Greiner and a picture of the car he was driving the night he was killed. "Did you see this guy or this car around here last week?"

She looked hard at the picture of Greiner and said, "No. And I'd remember an ugly mother fucker like that."

"What about the car? Do you remember seeing that?"

"The fuck I know about cars?" she said. That would have to do, Tom thought. He gave her the twenty and she turned and walked back to where she had been standing before. Tom noticed the other girls she had been with had moved away, probably out of a sense of self-preservation in case he had been a cop.

The scenario with the prostitute repeated itself two more times, roughly along the same lines, with the same results. Tom was starting to rethink his strategy. He couldn't afford to be passing out money for nothing all night and the people he was dealing with were not known for their civic mindedness. He was thinking about packing it in when he saw a familiar face on the corner of Genesee and East Parade.

It was Cherise, a hooker who had been around since Tom was a patrolman. Cherise was about 5' 10" and had mocha colored skin. She was wearing short shorts that exposed a pair of long toned legs. Tom knew she was a survivor. As long as he had known her she had avoided drugs and alcohol and she as cautious as she could be with the johns. She was quick with a smile but carried a switchblade in her shoulder bag that she wasn't afraid to use if she felt threatened. Tom also knew a secret she kept from most of her clientele. Cherise's real name was Charles. She was a transsexual. Charles' mother had kicked him out of the house when he was fifteen and he had been fending for himself/ herself ever since. The last Tom heard she was saving for hormone therapy and eventually the operation. The fact that she was still on the street made him wonder if she would ever be able to do it.

He pulled up to the curb and rolled down the window. She was talking on a cell phone and Tom knew she was pretending not to notice him. He waited until she shot him a glance and then she said into the phone, "I'll call you back Marcus." She walked over to the car and looked in. "Officer Donovan?"

"Yeah, well not officer anymore."

"Right. I heard about that business at the projects."

Tom said nothing to that. He never knew what people's reactions would be to his killing a drug dealer who had turned out to be unarmed. The firestorm that followed had acquired heavy racial overtones.

"What that man did to that poor girl, can't say that I'm sorry you did it," she added.

Not that it made Tom feel any better about it but at least he knew she wasn't going to hold it against him. She looked at him incredulously and asked, "You're not down here looking for a date are you?"

"Not really."

"Well then, what can I do for you, handsome?"

"Well, how about I do you a favor and then you do one for me," Tom said.

"Hmm, sounds kinky." She smiled and brushed a lock of dark hair off of her forehead.

"Not really," Tom interrupted. "There's a delivery van parked down at the edge of the park over your right shoulder."

Her face tensed up. She knew it wasn't good. "It's a van we impounded a couple of years ago. I'm guessing the vice squad is using it now."

"Are you shitting me?" she said.

"I shit you not. Since I don't want to get picked up for soliciting and you don't want to spend a night at the Holding Center, why don't you let me buy you a cup of coffee in about twenty minutes."

She pulled away slightly from his window. "I'll have tea."

"Okay. Meet me at the McDonald's around the corner in twenty. What I recommend you do after I drive away is call your friend Marcus back and hang out here for a few minutes. I doubt they'll follow you into the restaurant."

"Okay," she said and pulled out her phone.

"Don't stiff me Cherise," he said putting the car in gear.

"I'll be there darling."

<<<>>>

Twenty-five minutes later Cherise breezed into McDonald's and found Tom waiting in a booth with her tea. There were a handful of other people there. The man closest to them looked like he was homeless, totally absorbed in his coffee.

"I'm not happy about this Thomas," Cherise said as she slid into the booth across from him.

"Me either. This coffee tastes like ass."

"That's not what I meant. How's a girl supposed to make money when she's being harassed by the police, both past and present."

"Lift up your cup," he said. He raised his cup to his lips but then thought better of it.

There was a folded twenty-dollar bill under her cup. Cherise frowned and palmed it and slid it off the table. "My time is worth more than that," she said.

Tom shrugged and said, "Sorry, that's all I have. Besides this won't involve exchanging any bodily fluids."

Cherise put on a hurt expression. "That's not funny," she said.

"Sorry, that was a low blow. But I did probably save you from a night in the lockup."

She shuddered visibly. "They do not know how to treat a lady."

"I'm kinda surprised to see you're still out here Cherise."

She looked out the window as if she wanted to be somewhere else. Tom felt a twinge of guilt for the way he had teased her and now he had followed it up by prying.

"Well, you know," she explained, "I was taking some classes at ECC but it wasn't going too well."

They fell silent for a moment. Tom was curious, but felt he had already gotten too far into a subject that Cherise wasn't comfortable with. "Anyway—" he started. He took out the picture of

Greiner and the car and placed it on the table in front of her. "Have you ever seen this guy?"

She looked at the picture and immediately said, "That freak. Yeah, I saw him the night he got his head beat in."

Tom sat up. "Seriously? Was he cruising?"

She gazed at him and he was wondering if she was sorry she had told him. "Cherise this is important."

She closed her eyes and then opened them again. "Yeah," she said. "I talked to him for all of a minute and knew he wasn't right."

Tom opened up his palms prompting her to go on.

"You got to promise me that you won't tell anyone I told you this," she said almost under her breath.

"What is it?"

"He picked up Ally, Allison."

"Who is Allison?"

Cherise thoughtfully took the tea bag out of her cup and placed it on a napkin. "Little white girl. She's been working down here about six months. Poor little thing. I don't think she's long for this world."

"Have you seen her since that night?"

"No."

"Did you talk to the police?"

She shook her head and said, "Oh, they were down here like gangbusters for a few days after. Not just the locals either. Guys in suits from downtown and everything. Nobody told 'em anything." She put her finger on Greiner's picture. "We all figured he got what he deserved. Some old guy in a suit showed me the picture but I told him I had no idea why he would think I would know about such tawdry goings on."

So the cops probably had nothing, Tom thought. Given the nature of the crime, the history of the victim and the lack of witnesses they were probably ready to write it off as open/unsolved and move it to the back burner.

"Why do you care about this man?" Cherise asked him, bringing him back to the present.

He picked up the picture, folded it and put it in the pocket of his hoodie. "I really don't," he said. "Long story short I think the person who did this to him may be involved in another assault. Do you know where I can find Allison?"

She thought for a moment and then said, "She doesn't need anymore shit in her life right now."

"Cherise, I'm not a cop anymore and I'm not going to cause her any grief. I just want to talk to her."

"She lives with her scumbag boyfriend over the Arab market on Sycamore. I had to walk her home there one night after she got beat up by one of the other girls."

Tom gave up on the coffee and put the lid back on. He had a thought and asked, "You said you were trying to help her." He motioned towards her bag on the table. "Did you tell her how to defend herself?"

Cherise clutched the bag like it contained all of her secrets. "I tried. I think she had this rusty old razor."

That could explain the cuts that Greiner had sustained. First he gets cut by the girl and then he meets his fate with the business end of a blunt object. Just like Mark Krupp.

Tom stood up and Cherise did as well. It was in the bright florescent lights of the restaurant that you could see through the disguise. Out on the street she looked like any other working girl, maybe even better than most. In here though, Tom could see the razor stubble and the Adam's apple. On top of that Cherise looked tired, the cracks were starting to show.

"Take care of yourself," he said.

She touched his cheek. "You always were the gentleman." Then she turned serious and added, "Remember, you didn't hear any of this from me."

"Hand to God. We never had this conversation." He watched her turn and glide back in the direction of the ladies room.

<<<>>>

The Sycamore Market was easy enough to find. It was located near the intersection of Sycamore and Spruce in between two empty lots. It was larger that most of the neighborhood stores that dotted the area. (There wasn't a grocery chain that was willing to venture into this part of the city.) It was at least the width of two private homes and Tom counted eight windows on the second floor. The business itself was closed for the night, with an iron grate pulled across the front door. There was a separate entrance on the far left of the building. There was no doorbell or buzzer on the door so Tom pushed it open and found a staircase leading up to the apartments.

The smell of dampness and rotting wood permeated the space. The maroon paint on the walls was peeling off in sheets. The only light in the stairwell was a naked bulb at the top landing. Tom walked quietly up the stairs. At the top he came to an equally dingy hallway. The hallway ran down the back wall of the building and Tom strolled down looking for any kind of designation of who lived where without any luck. He had seen three mailboxes in the foyer without any names on them either. This wasn't the kind of place where you set down roots. When he reached the end of the hall and the last door he heard a crash.

"How the fuck are we supposed to eat if you won't get off your ass and go to work?" a voice yelled from inside the apartment.

He heard a girl's voice say something inaudible and then choke off a sob.

"Get up!" the man's voice yelled. He heard the girl howl like a wounded animal.

That was all he needed to hear. Even if it wasn't Allison he couldn't let this go, badge or no badge. The memory of a girl named Rachel Eberle flashed in his mind. Rachel had been an exotic dancer who had put herself in danger when she gave Tom information about the crooked people she worked for and had paid for it with her life. It was another red mark on Tom's ledger that he knew he would never be able to repay. He tried the knob and the door opened partway until the security chain stopped it.

The man must have heard the chain because he said, "What the fuck?"

Tom took a step back and waited until he saw the shadow under the door darken and the chain start to move. He had taken two steps back and now he rushed the door and threw his shoulder into it. There was a loud crack and the chain came off the doorjamb like it was made of balsa wood. The door moved a few inches and then slammed into whoever was standing behind it.

He stepped inside and surveyed the scene. There was a young girl, probably eighteen or so curled up in a ball in the middle of the squalid floor. To his right a tall skinny guy, probably in his late twenties was standing staring back at him with a dazed look on his face. He was covered with bad tattoos and had long greasy hair.

The man was shaking off the cobwebs and said, "What the fuck?"

"You really need to expand your vocabulary," Tom said looking at him.

The man was touching his forehead, probably where the door had hit him. He took a hard look at Tom and said, "You better have a warrant."

"Why would I need a warrant? I'm not a cop."

The tattooed man was getting his nerve back. He pointed at the door and said, "You better get the fuck out of here then."

Tom looked down at the girl. Her eyes were clenched shut. He could see a bruise on her cheek and it looked like her bottom lip was split open. He was pretty sure it was the girl he was looking for. He looked back at the man who was currently puffing himself up and said, "Nah. I think you should leave now."

The man looked at him in disbelief. "What?"

"Did I stutter?"

"This is my crib man! Nobody breaks in and kicks me out!"

"Relax pal. It's only temporary. Just until Ally grabs her stuff and we leave."

In his periphery Tom saw Allison stir at the mention of her name. She was still curled up in the fetal position but now she was looking at him warily.

The tattooed man was screaming now, "Fuck that and fuck you!" He apparently had heard enough because he started to move towards Tom. Tom had already balanced himself on the balls of his feet. As expected the kid had no plan, as soon as he was in range Tom flashed his left hand and it connected with the man's right eye, straightening him up. He followed that with a serious right just below the rib cage that knocked the wind out of him and doubled him over.

The man was gasping for air. Tom grabbed him by the hair, ran him out into the hallway and pushed him down on the dirty linoleum. He closed the door and took an old chair and braced it against the door. He turned to Allison, she hadn't moved but she was crying now. He walked over to her and said, "I can get you out of here if you want."

She said nothing, she just cried and now she was shaking. Tom jerked his thumb back towards the blockaded door and said, "You can stay with him if you want but I think you're smart enough to know that this is not going to end well."

"Where?" she murmured.

"There's a shelter on the West Side. They'll put you up for a few days. Then it's up to you. You can come back to this asshole if you want or anywhere else."

She sat up partially and whimpered, "I got nowhere else."

Tom crouched down to look into her tear-streamed face. "That's what I'm saying. I know you probably don't have a lot of options, but Allison I've seen this play out before and I can tell you, staying here isn't an option at all."

She looked at him and said nothing. She was pale and scrawny. Tom looked at her and thought that once she had been somebody's daughter, she'd gone to school and played with her friends. He wondered what happens to people between the dreams of childhood and what he saw in front of him now. His mind flashed to his own sister Colleen, who had died when she was ten years old. He held out his hand.

"C'mon," he said. "At least let me get you out of here tonight."

She held out a trembling hand and he helped her up.

While she was in the bedroom getting her things Tom went over to the door and opened it. Lover boy was nowhere in sight. He stuck his head out into the hallway and heard a commotion coming from an open door two apartments down. He could hear the tattooed man grunting and cursing and a woman screaming at him in a language he couldn't make out. He shut the door and turned to see Allison coming out of the bedroom with all of her worldly possessions stuffed into an old backpack. "Let's go," he said. He had his hand on the door and was about to open it when he spotted a cell phone on the floor by his foot. "Is that your phone?" he asked her.

She shook her head no. He picked it up and punched in 911. He told the operator that there was a home invasion in progress and gave the address. He threw the phone back on the floor and just for fun he crushed it under his boot heel.

When they turned into the hallway the tattooed man was exiting the neighbor's apartment with an old kitchen knife in his hand. He stopped and stared daggers at Tom. The neighbor was still screaming at him in Arabic but as soon as she could she slammed the door and they heard a deadbolt click.

"You want to try that shit now?" the man said.

Tom shook his head, "You're such a bad ass. As much as I would like to hang out here all night kicking the shit out of you I really need to get out of here before the cops come."

"You ain't going nowhere."

"Really we gotta run. I already called. Sorry about your phone," Tom said. The man looked at him, confused and then looked around Tom in Allison's direction.

"Ally, this is bullshit!" he shouted. He took a step towards them.

Tom reached up under his sweatshirt and pulled the 9mm off his belt. The man looked at it in disbelief. "I've had an ass-full of you already," Tom said. "Drop the knife and get on your knees with your hands on your head."

There was the sound of a siren in the distance and the man stood stunned. Tom raised the gun and pointed it at him. His stomach churned but he fought it off. "I said get on your knees," he growled.

The man finally moved, somewhat reluctantly. He set the knife down and then knelt. Tom, never lowering the gun, guided Allison past him and then as he went by swung the Glock as hard as he could striking the man in the side of the head. The man went the rest of the way to the floor in a heap.

As they drove slowly down Sycamore Tom looked in his rearview mirror and saw the lights from at least three patrol cars converging on the building.

Chapter 20

Allison didn't speak or move at first; she just stared at the dashboard. Tom wondered if she was in shock. After he put some distance between them and the apartment he pulled into an all night mini-mart.

"I'm starving," he said. "Do you want anything?"

She looked at him with vacant eyes as if he were speaking a foreign language.

"I'll grab you something," he said.

He turned off the car and took the keys, leaving nothing to chance. There wasn't too much in the store that looked like it was safe to consume but he found a couple of ham sandwiches and two cans of soda. He also found a roll of gauze and a tube of antiseptic for Allison's lip. He remembered he had spent all of his cash on prostitutes earlier so he had to put it on his credit card.

When he returned to the car it looked like Allison hadn't moved. If anything it looked like she was trying to disappear into her worn leather jacket. Tom started the car and turned on the heater. He tore off a piece of the gauze and offered it to her. "Put this on your lip," he said.

She took the gauze tentatively from him and winced when she dabbed at her lip. He took one of the cold cans of soda and offered it to her. "Hold this on there for a while."

"Who are you?" she asked quietly.

"To tell you the truth, I was looking for you."

She seemed to tense at that and he saw her hand reaching for the door latch.

"I just need to ask you some questions."

He saw fear in her eyes. She looked like she was about to bail out.

"Allison, I'm going to take you to the shelter. I meant that. I just want to ask you about the other night."

She eased slightly, either that or she was too tired to run. She continued looking at him but now with a look that was part confusion, part curiosity. "What?" she started.

"About the John you were with the other night."

The fear came back and she shook her head. Tom knew she was preparing to lie to him.

"I'm not a cop and you're not in trouble," he said as reassuringly as possible. "I take it you haven't talked to the cops."

"No," she said. "I haven't left the apartment since that night. That's why Evan was beating on me."

"This guy, the John. He scared the shit out of you?"

She set her jaw and wiped a tear off her cheek, "Fucking creep. He hit me–like it was my fault he couldn't get it up. Then he grabbed me and I thought he was going to strangle me so I cut him."

"What happened after you cut him?"

She shuddered a little. "I just wanted to nick him, you know? Scare him... but he got mad and when I tried to get out of the car he grabbed me and was holding me on the ground."

"How did you get away?"

She looked at Tom and said, "That's when the other guy hit him."

She took the can and gauze away from her mouth and looked at it. This latest degradation she had suffered seemed to derail her train of thought because she shook with a sob and started crying again.

Tom took a different picture out of his pocket. He unfolded a picture of Phil Benzinger and showed it to her.

"Ally... I need you to look at this."

She put the gauze back on her lip and wiped her eyes with her other hand. He turned on the dome light so she could get a better look. She studied it for a moment and Tom observed her. Nothing seemed to be registering.

"Was this the guy who hit him?" Tom asked.

She stared at the picture for a moment and then said, "No..."

"Are you sure?"

She looked at Tom with a little anger. "Yeah," she pointed at the picture. "That guy is too old."

With his theory now shot to hell Tom pressed on nonetheless. "Do you remember what he looked like?"

"I was scared shitless," she said. He was wearing a dark hoodie and I couldn't really see his face that well."

"But you're sure this isn't the guy?" Tom asked, holding up the picture of Benzinger.

"That guy is too old. I could tell that much at least."

"Did he say anything to you?"

She sighed and said, "He helped me up and asked if I was okay. I couldn't answer him, I was so scared. Something about the look in his eyes... he scared me too.

"Did he say anything?" Tom asked.

Allison nodded. "He just said, 'That's all I can do. You have to save yourself now.'"

Tom drove Allison to the shelter on Plymouth Avenue. He had to ring the bell three times before the lady in charge would even open the door. It took him another twenty minutes to talk her into letting Allison in. The shelter was full and understaffed at the moment. But after hearing Allison's story they couldn't turn her away. Tom left his business card with the administrator and told them to call if Allison wanted to talk or caused them any grief.

On the way home he thought about Allison. He had decided not to give her a lecture on making better decisions. Not that he didn't care but he had seen this scenario too many times before and felt resigned to the fact that she had either heard all of it before and was bent on self destruction anyway or she was beyond help. He truly hoped that a few nights off the streets might convince her she had to 'save herself.'

It wasn't Benzinger. So why would he try to scare Sherry off? Maybe there was another person, lurking around in the shadows, picking off all of these miscreants. Was it the same person who had crushed Mark Krupp's skull? If only he had access to the medical examiner's reports, he could compare the damage that had been inflicted in the similar assaults.

It was pushing 2:00 AM and suddenly he felt exhausted. He headed for home with all of this on his mind when he remembered he still had Whitey's problems to deal with the next day.

Chapter 21

After a restless night's sleep, Tom was up at 9:15. He checked his phone to make sure Whitey hadn't called. He called Bob Stanley, the attorney, and apologized for not getting back to him sooner. Tom cringed when Stanley evenly told him that he had to go with someone else on a matter, but he would probably have something for him next week. Tom apologized again and said he would call on Monday.

With nothing else to do but wait for Whitey to call, Tom booted up his laptop. Something in his gut told him that Phil Benzinger had an interest in the files that Sherry had been looking into. Tom wanted to take a harder look at the ex-deputy. He pulled up the copy of the disciplinary report that Barlow had sent him. He had been charged with menacing and the complainant was listed as Nicholas Atkins.

Tom opened up his public records program and found Nick Atkins in under a minute. He was twenty-six years old, his profession was listed as 'musician' and he had a criminal record for assault, possession and public lewdness, the kind of guy any sheriff's deputy would love to see courting his daughter. There was also currently a court order warning him not to contact one Kelsey Benzinger, obviously the daughter. A search on Kelsey brought up next to nothing. She had recently moved from the city back to the suburbs. A quick check told Tom that she had moved back in with her parents.

Just out of curiosity, Tom did a general web search on Nick Atkins and eventually found himself on Atkin's band's web site. The name of the band was Fall From Mercy and to Donovan they looked like a bunch of losers. He found a picture of Atkins, on stage, shirtless and screaming into a microphone. There were links to a few of the bands songs on the site and Tom cued one up. To him it sounded like they only knew two or three chords and the vocals were mostly screaming. He turned it off halfway through the song.

Again, he found himself wondering if he was getting old. He could see why Benzinger would be less than thrilled with his daughter's choice of men. Not only was this guy a punk but his band was for shit too. He wondered what kind of self-esteem issues Kelsey Benzinger must have had to hook up with this clown.

That brought him back to Phil Benzinger and the matter at hand. On the one hand, he had motivation from his personal life to be angry. The call out of the blue to Sherry, warning her to mind her own business was a red flag too. On the other hand, the only eyewitness he had was sure that Benzinger wasn't her avenging angel. And then there was the thought that none of this had anything to do with Mark Krupp, the reason Tom had gotten involved in the first place. Tom tried to figure out what his own motivation was in all this. Was part of him still trying to be a cop? Or was there something else below the surface that made him want justice for an innocent man.

Whatever his motivation, he was out of ideas, for now.

Tom was starting to get anxious so he called Whitey Brennan. "Anything yet?" he asked.

"Not a word," Whitey grumped. "I've been sitting here staring at this damned phone all day."

"Well, I'm not doing anything either so I suppose I'll come and wait with you."

Tom was almost to his car when his mother called him.

"What did you say to your uncle?" she asked immediately.

Shit, not now, Tom thought. "Why, what did he say?"

"He accused me of using you to plead my case."

"Mom, you know that's not true. I just gave him my honest opinion."

Rose sighed and then said, "Well he's still being a *minchione* about the whole thing."

"A what?"

"Never mind," Rose said. "I feel like I'm fifteen again! I'm waiting for him to ground me."

Tom climbed into his car and said, "Mom, give him a couple of days. I'll talk to him again if you think it would help."

Rose didn't reply at once but Tom could hear her breathing. "It's going to be alright," he added. "I like Tony, you like Tony. I'm pretty sure Sam will come around."

She seemed to be mildly placated so after he promised to drop by after the weekend they broke the connection.

True to his word Whitey was upstairs in his office looking at the pre paid cell phone on his desk when Tom arrived. There was a new addition to the room, a flat screen television, mounted on the wall. It was on with the volume down. Whitey looked up when Tom entered and shook his head. "Still nothing," he said.

"Do you have the money?" Tom asked, pulling up a chair.

"I do... Christ Tom, that's a lot of money."

"Well, I have a plan. And if it works like I hope it does we'll get it back tonight."

Whitey peered at him with a look of incredulity. "Get it back?" he asked.

Tom explained what he had in mind. All the while Whitey's facial expression never changed. He looked at Tom for a moment after he had finished and then said, "I suppose that could work."

They settled in to wait. Whitey turned up the volume on the TV slightly. He had the outdoor channel on. Whitey and his sons were avid hunters and he stared at the image of two men field dressing a large buck. Tom wasn't sure if Whitey was absorbed in the program or was preoccupied with the thought of giving away twenty-five grand to a blackmailer. For some reason the vision of the two men pulling out the deer's insides made Whitey ask, "Are you hungry lad?"

"Starving," Tom said, looking away from the TV.

Whitey called downstairs to the bar and ordered a couple of sandwiches. About fifteen minutes later there was a knock on the door.

"Come in," Whitey said.

The door opened and Jack O'Neill walked in carrying two take out containers. He looked surprised to see Tom. "I didn't know you had company," he said.

"Thanks, Jackie. Just set 'em on the table over there."

O'Neill set the containers down and moved towards the door. Tom noticed he glanced back once in his direction.

After they ate Tom asked Whitey if he could use his computer to do a little more research on the other matter he was working on. He spent the better part of two hours coming up with nothing he didn't already know. Whitey had gotten up to give Tom access to the computer and moved to an armchair that Tom thought may have come from his late grandfather's house. Whitey had given up on the outdoor channel and surfed until he settled on an old black and white movie.

Tom was leaning back in the chair, rubbing his fatigued eyes when Whitey said, "What a load of crap."

Tom looked across the room at him. "What's that?" he asked.

"Have you ever seen this film? *Boy's Town*?"

"No... "

Whitey Chuckled without much mirth. "Spencer Tracy, Mickey Rooney. Pretty famous movie."

Tom shook his head and shrugged.

Whitey went on, "All I can say is maybe that's how reform schools were in 1939, but it was a whole new ball game by the time I got there."

Tom had never really known anything about Whitey's formative years until Whitey had recently told him about them. He had no idea what kind of memories and scars an institutionalized childhood had left on him.

"There was no Father Flanagan at Stafford..." Whitey said retreating back into his melancholy.

The cell phone on the desk started chirping. Tom and Whitey sat frozen for a moment and then Whitey stood up and walked towards the desk. Whitey fumbled for the call button, found it and said, "Hello."

Tom waved to get his attention and mouthed the word "speaker."

Whitey squinted at the phone and found the appropriate button. As he set the phone back on the desk between them Tom heard the heavily distorted voice.

"...even think about telling me you don't have the money." He caught the end of the sentence. You could get a voice changer on line for around twelve dollars. Tom had wondered about the market for a product like that. What honest, law abiding person would have a need for one. Well, here was the answer.

"I've got it," Whitey said flatly.

"Be at the Tifft Nature Preserve in fifteen minutes. Then wait for a call. Come alone. No bullshit."

Whitey started to say something but the line went dead.

"Goddamn it!" he yelled.

Tom was up and grabbed a small duffel bag he had brought with him. "Where's your car?" he asked.

"Out back," Whitey said.

"Good. Let's go."

Chapter 22

Whitey had recently traded in his fourteen year old Cadillac for a newer model. It had leather seats, climate control, satellite radio and a spacious trunk. The trunk was an important feature because Donovan had been riding in it ever since they left the back lot of the tavern. He didn't want to take any chances in case they were being watched. He was lying on his back trying to stay as comfortable as possible. He had his mag light in one hand and his cell in the other.

"We're here," Whitey's voice came over his phone. Tom had instructed him to stay on the line with him while he waited for the call on the throw away phone. "Five minutes to spare."

"Good," Tom replied. He rolled his shoulders and tried to move around to stay loose. Even though the car had an excellent ride, traveling in the trunk left a lot to be desired.

The other phone chirped and Tom heard Whitey answer it. He could only hear Whitey's end of the conversation.

"What?" he heard him say. "But... no..."

Then Whitey raised his voice. Tom was afraid he was going to lose it. "Listen here you fuck," Whitey started to say. Then Tom heard nothing for a moment. Finally he heard Whitey again, "Okay... okay, I got it."

There was no sound for a moment and then Tom said in a near whisper, "Whitey?"

"I'm here."

"What's going on?" He heard the transmission shift into gear.

"Apparently this was a test. We have to take the money to Cazenovia Park."

"Shit," Tom said. Where in the park?"

"They said at the corner of Potter and Peconic there's a fire hydrant. Thirty feet into the park there's an elm tree with a hole near the base. They told me to leave it there and then go back to the bar."

Tom racked his memory, trying to recall the layout of the park. He'd grown up in the neighborhood and played little league baseball there as a boy.

"Whitey," he said. "Listen, when you're driving along the edge of the park there is a bend in Potter road before you get to Peconic. Make sure nobody is behind us and slow down. And tell me when we're almost there."

"Okay."

Ten minutes later Tom sensed the car slowing. "Get ready," he heard Whitey say.

"Were we followed?" Tom asked.

"Don't think so. I took an indirect route and made a few extra turns. There's nobody behind us."

"Pop the trunk," Tom said. Then he jammed his phone into his jacket pocket. The car came to a halt and Tom heard the latch click open. As quickly as he could he grabbed his bag, climbed out of the car and then quickly closed the lid. He had broken the light bulb in the trunk, to Whitey's mild displeasure, when he was trying to disable it, so it wouldn't throw off any light. He hustled over to the short fence and went over it while he heard the Caddy accelerate.

He cut deeper into the park, which was technically closed, determined to stay off the dimly lit path. He made his way as quickly as he could, not wanting to trip over a stray tree root and do a face plant in the dirt. He covered about a hundred yards and found a cluster of trees. He looked off to his left and could see the taillights of the Cadillac about thirty yards away. This was probably the best spot.

He pulled out his phone and said, "Go." Then he knelt down and opened the bag. He pulled out the thermal vision field glassed that he had picked up from Barlow security that day on his way to Donovan's. Barlow had an impressive collection of surveillance equipment that Tom had never seen used. The equipment reminded him that he didn't know everything about Rod Barlow's business dealings. He took out the Glock and tucked it into the waistband of his black pants. He hoped to God he wouldn't have to use it, but better safe than sorry. Raising the glasses to his eyes, at first all he saw was a bright blur. There was a good deal of light coming from Potter Road and the homes on the other side. He adjusted his aim and saw Whitley's silhouette moving into the park and approaching the elm tree. He took a quick look around for other people. He couldn't fathom having to explain why he was lying in the middle of a group of trees in the park with binoculars and a loaded weapon.

Tom looked back through the glasses just in time to see Whitey drive off and turn left onto Peconic. He swept the park in all directions and saw no one.

Forty-five minutes later and nothing had happened. A few cars had passed by the spot on Potter Road without stopping. A man had ridden by on a bike and done the same. The park itself was totally deserted. The only time Tom's pulse rate went up was when a police car cruised past, sweeping his location with the spotlight mounted on the driver's side door. He had managed to make himself invisible by crouching down and staying motionless while the light penetrated the trees.

The tedium brought him back to his days as a cop. He'd been on numerous stakeouts outside of drug houses and other spots. This was different though; he wasn't sitting in an unmarked car with a radio and backup around the corner. He had perspired in the trunk and now he was chilled from the damp ground and cool air.

His phone buzzed and he cursed silently. The light of the phone shined like a beacon in his almost pitch black hiding spot.

"What?" he hissed into the phone.

"It's off," Whitey said.

"What?"

"I came back to the bar and waited like they said to. They just called and said I fucked up and I was going to be sorry."

Tom panicked briefly and looked all around him. Nothing stirred or made a sound.

"Shit," he said. "Somebody must have seen me."

"I don't know Tommy," Whitey sounded crestfallen.

Tom thought for a second and then said, "I'm going to go get the money. Come down here and pick me up by the hydrant."

<<<>>>

Riding back in the Cadillac Whitey was angry. "I don't understand," he said. "I don't know how they could have seen us. There wasn't a soul around."

"Maybe they saw you talking on your own phone," Tom offered.

Whitey shook his head, "I had it in my lap the whole time... shit, I was so careful."

They fell silent. They had been careful. He knew that one of the reasons that his grandfather had made Whitey a trusted confidante and part of his business was that Whitey wasn't stupid, he didn't miss much.

They rode in silence the rest of the way to the Tavern. Whitey was about to pull around the side when he slammed on the brakes and cursed. Tom followed Whitey's gaze to the front door of the tavern, which was now closed for the evening. There was an envelope taped to the front door.

Whitey took his foot off the brake and pulled up to the curb. They both jumped out of the car. Instinctively Tom looked up and down the street on the odd chance they were being watched while Whitey retrieved the envelope. He opened it up and took out a single sheet of paper. He turned pale when he looked at it in the light from the street lamp.

"What is it?" Tom asked, walking over to him.

Whitey said nothing. He grimaced and handed the paper to Tom. Tom held it out to where the nearest streetlight was shining down. There were two pictures on it, one of a tree lined marsh and the other of a heavily rusted old gardening spade. There was a message scrawled on the bottom of the page. All it said was;

"YOU WERE WARNED."

Chapter 23

Whitey was in a sour mood. He sat behind his desk with two fingers of whiskey that he hadn't touched since he poured it. The only light on in the room was the desk lamp and Tom was looking at Whitey's furrowed brow as he stared down at the pictures.

"Are those legitimate?" Tom asked.

"That was forty years ago Tom," Whitey said looking up. "It could be bullshit but I can't say for sure, and I can't take for granted that whoever is doing this knows enough about it that they're not."

They fell silent again. Whitey absentmindedly picked up the tumbler and downed the contents in one gulp. He shuddered and coughed slightly. Tom had declined a drink. The adrenaline had long since worn off and he was exhausted after the last few nights worth of adventures.

"I don't understand," Whitey said. "We were so careful. How did they know you were in the park?"

"Someone's watching you."

Whitey stared at him. He suddenly reached for the remote and turned the TV on. Then he turned the volume up loud. Tom looked at him quizzically and then Whitey grabbed the paper in front of him and picked up a pen and then wrote something down. He finished and turned the paper around. There was one word on it; *"Bugged?"*

Tom didn't think so but he just shrugged. Then he motioned for Whitey to come outside with him. When they got far enough away from the building he said, "I'm not sure, but just to be safe I can get a bug detector from the same place I got the binoculars and sweep your office. In the meantime don't say a word to anybody and if you have to call me use your cell and don't call me from the bar."

Tom made it home just after three AM and collapsed into bed. If he dreamed he didn't remember it. He awoke after ten the next morning with a headache and stiff legs from crouching in the trees at the park the night before.

After administering some caffeine into his blood stream he checked his email. There was a group message from Rod Barlow reminding his people about the concert that night. There was a reminder that anyone who was licensed to do so could "bring a friend."

He spent the morning half heartedly cleaning his apartment and catching up on his laundry. He was feeling lethargic in the afternoon so he went to the gym to try to get his blood pumping and clear his mind.

At five PM Tom was at Barlow security with nine other men, being briefed by Rod Barlow on what was expected of them that night at the concert. The management of the company that had been hired to do security initially had gotten nervous after hearing reports of trouble at other venues on the tour. There were fights backstage, rampant drug use and a problem with counterfeit backstage passes popping up. Plus none of their people were armed and at one of the venues someone had been caught trying to bring a gun through the backstage door. He knew Rod from being in the same business and asked if he could help. Barlow was more than happy to help out for a fair price.

When Barlow had finished with his instructions he distributed bright yellow windbreakers with the word 'security' emblazoned across the front and back.

"Your visibility is a deterrent," he said to stifle the groaning. "Also, if you're carrying it will cover it up, and if you are not carrying, they'll think you are."

Tom tried his on. It was a few sizes too big. He thought about saying something but changed his mind. Did it really matter how well a glow-in-the-dark yellow jacket fit?

The talent was predictably late arriving to the arena. There were six different acts and all of them seemed to have a small army for an entourage. Tom and the rest of the crew from Barlow Security were stationed at the stage door with metal detecting wands and scanners to check for bogus backstage credentials. The first few hours were busy but went without a hitch. After all of the talent and their people had been checked off by the promoter the Barlow people were allowed to rove the area in pairs. Tom was paired with Darryl Toms, an off duty Buffalo policeman. They took up a spot near the dressing rooms and kept their eyes open.

The music was loud and the beat seemed nonstop. The performers all seemed to be dressed for the part. Tom wondered how many of them were really nice kids from the suburbs playing dress up. He knew the real killers were out on the street.

After a while the tedium made his mind wander. He started thinking about Whitey's situation. The more he thought about the idea of someone having the wherewithal and nerve to bug the tavern the more absurd it seemed. The answer had to be simpler. Something was out of place. Hugh had been up to his eyeballs in questionable activities and with the exception of the State Police cracking down on his bookmaking operation in the '80's had never had anyone even get close to disrupting his business or extorting money from him. What were they missing?

It dawned on him then, the one variable from Hugh's time in charge to Whitey's. Tom had seen it with his own eyes the day before and now it made perfect sense.

Chapter 24

Tom hadn't gotten home from the concert until 3:30 AM. He was wired though and couldn't really sleep. He gave up on the idea at 8:30 AM and called Whitey. They arranged to meet at Whitey's house at ten. They were having coffee in Whitey's sunroom and Tom pitched his idea.

"Are you sure?" Whitey asked.

"Well, ninety-five percent sure," Tom replied.

"How can you tell?"

"Even with the voice scrambled, the tone, the pitch, the way the person pronounced certain words. I don't think I'm wrong."

"A woman?"

"Yeah," Tom nodded.

At four PM there were a handful of people in the dimly lit Tavern despite the fact that it was a perfect day outside. Whitey was standing at the end of the bar when his cell phone started ringing.

"Yeah..." he said into the phone. "What... is she?" He half turned away and shielded the phone with his hand. After listening for another moment he said, "Alright, tell Peter to get ready. I'll pick you up in five minutes." He ended the call and looked at Jack O'Neill, who was behind the bar. "I gotta go take care of something Jackie. Hold down the fort."

"Will do," O'Neill replied.

Whitey went out the front door and disappeared. Jack checked to make sure everyone's glass was full and stepped out from behind the bar and through the swinging door into the kitchen. He dug out his phone and punched in a number.

"C'mon..." he said waiting for the call to be picked up. Then, "It's me... I think we have a problem." He listened and then cut off the other person. "He knows where you are," he said trying to keep his voice down. "I don't know... all I know is he's meeting his sons and they're in an awful hurry..." Jack looked up and saw he wasn't alone in the kitchen.

"Hello Jack," Tom said. The sound of a woman's voice yelling over the open line went on until Jack recovered and ended the call. Tom had silently walked into the kitchen on Jack's heels.

"What the fuck do you want?" O'Neill asked him.

"Seriously?" Tom said shaking his head. "You want to do it this way?"

O'Neill sneered at him. "I don't know what you're going on about but you're about to get your ass kicked."

Tom exhaled and said, "Give me your phone."

O'Neill grinned and stuffed the phone in his pants pocket. "You used to be a pretty tough guy, running around with a badge and a gun. Why don't you come and take it from me."

Whitey had entered the kitchen through the back door. Before Jack knew what was happening, Whitey grabbed him and threw him chest first into the old butcher block table. Jack hit the table hard and rolled over it and onto the floor. He was trying to get up on his hands and knees when Whitey grabbed him by the hair with his left hand and brought his right fist down on the base of Jack's skull. Jack went back down in a heap. He was conscious, but barely. Tom came around the table with a roll of duct tape.

"Dan and Peter?" Tom asked.

Whitey's face was flushed and he looked like he was ready to kill. It took a moment for the question to register and then he looked at Tom, who was trussing up O'Neill with the tape. "They're on the way," he said.

Tom had convinced Whitey that the time had come to bring in some help so Whitey had reluctantly told his sons the story. To his surprise they didn't seem fazed in the least.

It was a gamble to be sure. The shovel and the body were still hanging over Whitey's head. But Tom had convinced himself that if he was right about Jack O'Neill, this was their best play. Now they had leverage. The big question was though, how much leverage did they have? How important was O'Neill to his conspirators?

Donovan was also leery that they may have to resort to extracting information from O'Neill. The plan was to take him to Whitey's hunting cabin in Cattaraugus County and the boys would sit on him until the situation was resolved. Whitey had been a huge part of Hugh's world and Tom knew he had killed and watched people be killed before. Add the fact that O'Neill had been spying on him as part of a blackmail scheme and Tom knew O'Neill could be in for a world of hurt.

Chapter 25

Monday morning Tom was reading through an affidavit that Bob Stanely had sent him regarding a case he was handling. A client of Stanley's was accused of leaving the scene of an accident on a residential street in Orchard Park. Stanley wanted Tom to go to the scene, take pictures and see if he could talk to the two witnesses listed on the police report or better yet, find another witness who was a little more sympathetic to his client.

He tried to call Whitey and got the recorded message that Whitey's phone was out of service. The cabin was in a remote wooded part of Cattaraugus and the cell reception was spotty at best. He called the tavern and found out that Whitey's son Dan was there.

"No news yet Tommy," Dan told him. "He hasn't said a word since they got there." After Tom asked a few more questions Dan cut him off. "We'll call you when we hear something." Tom hadn't noticed it before but Dan was starting to sound like his father.

Tom cringed. He knew Whitey's patience would only last so long. And he had seen first hand Whitey's handiwork with the section of rubber hose with the lead weight in it.

So he left for Orchard Park, where he would spend the better part of the day taking pictures of the accident scene and knocking on doors. The few people who were home at the time eyed him suspiciously and said they had seen nothing. Tom didn't consider any of it time well spent but it was what Stanley had asked for.

He got home that afternoon and e-mailed the pictures and report to Stanley. He considered driving down to Whitey's hunting cabin but ruled that out. He knew he wouldn't be any help at this point and there was also a part of him that didn't want to know what was going on. There was one beer left in his refrigerator; he popped the top and took it out to the front porch. The porch was sparsely furnished to say the least; there were two lawn chairs and a rickety old end table. It was a perfect June afternoon though and Tom sat down and listened to the sounds of the unseen cars driving up and down Elmwood.

He saw Caroline pull up to the curb across the street with Brandon. She was dressed in slacks and a blue blouse like she had just got out of work and she was carrying a bag of groceries. She and Brandon crossed the street without looking up and seeing him. Tom thought she looked tired and sad. He heard the front door open and close and then he started thinking about her brother Mark again.

All of the conjecture and the legwork that he and Sherry had put in had got him no closer to finding out what really happened the night that Mark had his head bashed in. He had told Caroline and her father that he would look into it but now he realized he had gotten sidetracked in a quagmire of other people's shit. With nothing to do but wait for some kind of news from the cabin or the black mailer, he was free to refocus on Mark Krupp. He decided to go back to the start.

He waited to give Caroline enough time to get settled before going downstairs. When he knocked on her door she had just finished cleaning up after dinner and Brandon was in the kitchen doing his homework. Caroline had made coffee and they took it into the living room.

"We need to figure out what Mark was doing there," Tom said.

Caroline thought for a moment and then said, "That's what I don't understand. Dad had hired a lawyer for him and the lawyer told him to stay away from Jennifer until the custody hearing.

The lawyer said that he'd found a few things that he could use to show that she was an unfit parent but he just needed more time."

Tom looked at Caroline. She had seemed relaxed at first but now dredging all of this up seemed to be reflected in her face and voice. He had a thought and said, "His phone..."

"They never found it," she finished his thought. "His wallet and his phone were taken."

"I wonder if there was anything on his phone that would explain why he would do something so rash?" Tom wondered.

"Dad called the carrier when he was in the hospital. They told him no one had used the phone after the night Mark was mugged."

Tom stopped with the coffee cup halfway to his mouth. "The phone company told him that?"

Caroline scrunched up her brow. "Yeah... why?"

"The wireless companies usually only give out that information to the person whose name is on the account."

"Oh," she said. "Well, dad was helping Mark out with some of his bills." She frowned again. "Jen never went back to work after Alexis was born. And, we found out that she was neck deep in debt before she got her hooks into Mark. Mark never asked for help but my dad knew he needed a little. He put Mark and Jennifer on his family plan."

"I need to talk to your father," Tom said.

<<<>>>

Late the next afternoon Tom was waiting in his car in the church parking lot of Our Lady Help of Christians in Cheektowaga. He was parked near the chapel and shrine that had been erected in 1852 by an immigrant, Joseph Batt, who pledged that he would do so if the ship he and is family were on would make it through a storm and reach America safely. The shrine drew pilgrims for years after that, mostly immigrants or the children of immigrants celebrating their safe passage to America. Even after the trolley line cut off service at the city line the pilgrimage was finished on foot by the faithful. Thirty yards from the Shrine was a mausoleum that looked much more modern. The whole area had a somber feel to it.

Detective Ray Nightingale arrived, ten minutes late, in an unmarked car. He pulled up alongside Tom's car and rolled the window down. He already looked agitated.

"So what's with all the clandestine bull shit?" he growled.

"I need to show you something and I wanted to keep it quiet," Tom replied.

"Yeah, I got that. I suppose you're going to tell me you solved the case of the battered wife beater."

Tom was unfazed. He couldn't think of a better option even though he knew convincing Nightingale would be an uphill battle. "Look," he said, "just give me ten minutes and take a look. If you decide it's bullshit then you tell me to piss off and never hear from me again." Tom got out of his car and handed Nightingale a piece of paper.

Nightingale pulled a face and then took a pair of reading glasses out of the pocket of his sport coat. "What is it?" he asked.

"It's a printout of calls and texts from Jennifer and Mark Krupp's cell phones.

He looked over his glasses at Tom and said, "Where did you get this."

"It's all perfectly legal. Mark Krupp's father is the administrator of the account. He gave it to me."

Nightingale frowned again and looked like he was about to tell Tom to take a hike.

Tom said, "Just look at the calls that are highlighted."

Nightingale reluctantly did. "And?" he asked.

"The night Mark got rolled there were three calls from Jennifer's phone to his. Then one from his to hers."

The wheels were turning in Nightingale's head but he wasn't about to give in. "So what does that prove?"

"She set him up," Tom said.

Nightingale shook his head. "That's a stretch" he started to say.

"And there is somebody else involved," Tom interrupted.

"And who would that be?"

"There are numerous other calls from Jennifer's phone to a third number. I highlighted three of them. Two the night of the mugging and one a couple of days later when I happened to be at her apartment."

Nightingale bristled at that. "What the hell were you doing there?" he asked.

Tom didn't back down. "What I was hired to do."

"You, my friend, are a private citizen. If you think you can go around sticking your nose..."

Tom cut him off again. "Yeah I get it. I was a cop once too and I know what you think about P.I.s.

Maybe Mark Krupp was the biggest piece of shit on the planet and he deserved to have his head cracked open. The fact is you've got somebody running around whacking people on the head and chances are he's done it before and he's going to do it again."

They fell silent and stared at each other. Tom half expected the detective to throw his evidence back in his face and drive off but Nightingale surprised him and took another look at the paper.

"Besides," Tom went on. "This isn't the first time Jenny Krupp has tried to game the system."

Nightingale looked up at Tom with a puzzled expression. Then he tapped the paper with his finger. "Okay, so who does this other number belong to?"

"I don't have a name on that yet, but I'm betting I know who it is."

<<<>>>

Tom waited until it was dark and then made his way over to David Avenue. He parked as close as he could to the Krupp's apartment and rang the bell. Through the glass in the front door he saw Jennifer coming down the stairs dressed in tight jeans and a t-shirt with the word 'pink' on it. When she got to the bottom of the stairs she looked through the window at him in surprise. She must have been expecting someone else. She hesitantly opened the door a few inches and asked, "What do you want?"

"To confess," Tom replied.

She glared at him for a second and then tried to shut the door. Tom stuck his foot in and held it open. "I guess you figured out I'm not from the insurance company," he said."

"His bitch sister sent you, didn't she?" she hissed.

"Yeah, but that's not why I'm here," Tom said. "I'm here because of what their lawyer told me..."

Jenny put all her weight into closing the door on Tom's foot. "... about you," he finished.

She looked angry and he knew he had accomplished what he had come to do. He put pressure on the door from his side and pulled his shoe out. As soon as he was clear she slammed the door shut. "Fuck off!" She yelled through the glass and then ran upstairs.

Tom wondered if he'd overdone it. He didn't want a concerned neighbor calling the police. He backed off the porch and went back across the street to his car. He climbed in and looked up at Jenny's window just in time to see the curtains open and then close.

The street was deserted and only a few of the houses seemed to have any lights on. Tom waited for fifteen minutes until he saw a pair of headlights approaching in his rearview mirror. He got out of his car, moved to the front and leaned on the fender. He glanced up at the apartment again. Jenny had turned off her lights but he saw the curtains move again. The other car slowed and pulled to the curb behind his. The driver killed the lights and got out.

"Officer Seifert," Tom said. Seifert was off duty and dressed in civilian clothes. His whole look though still screamed cop, the weightlifter's arms and the military style haircut.

"You don't learn, do you?" Seifert said taking a few steps forward.

Tom stood up and faced him. "Oh, but I have. I've learned quite a bit about your girlfriend up there." He gestured towards the apartment.

"Listen smartass..." Seifert started.

"This is what happens when a guy lets the wrong head do the thinking," Tom said, speaking over Seifert.

Seifert fell silent. He looked at Tom and took a furtive glance up at Jenny's apartment as if the answer he wanted was up there.

"She's going to ruin you," Tom said, getting Seifert's attention back. "If she hasn't already," he added.

Seifert seemed to be considering his next move. His face clouded over in the dim light and then he reached behind him and pulled out his service weapon. He didn't raise it. He just held it at his side and stared at Tom.

"Whoa, no need for that," Tom said. He raised his hands and showed Seifert that he was only holding his phone.

Seifert tried to look menacing, but Tom could tell there wasn't much behind it. "I warned you once," the young cop said. "You are really starting to piss me off."

"Piss you off enough to pull out your weapon on an unarmed man while you're off duty?" Tom asked.

"I don't know what you think you're doing but..." Seifert paused when he heard the sound of a car coming up the street behind him. The driver had been running without his lights on but now turned them on. Seifert froze for a second and then awkwardly stuffed the gun down the front of his pants. The car stopped right behind him and the headlights made it hard to see. There was the sound of a door opening.

"Officer Seifert! Turn around!" Ray Nightingale said loudly.

Seifert slowly turned around and faced the headlights. Tom saw Nightingale's silhouette walking up to face them.

"What the fuck have you done?" Nightingale barked.

"Ray..." Seifert sputtered. "This guy..."

"Never mind that," Nightingale snapped. "On second thought, maybe you should shut the fuck up for now and carefully consider your options here. Oh, and what's this 'Ray' shit? It's Detective Nightingale to you."

Chapter 26

Earlier that evening, in another quiet place, Phil Benzinger walked along a tree-lined roadway at Forest Lawn Cemetery. It was approaching dusk, the sun barely making it through the foliage. A breeze rustled the leaves drowning out the sound of traffic from Delaware Avenue. The sprawling 269-acre burial ground held more than 160,000 graves, including those of President Millard Fillmore, Red Jacket the Seneca Indian chief and the singer Rick James. He'd noticed all of the elaborate headstones and sculptures that adorned the cemetery before, but tonight he was too preoccupied to play the part of tourist.

Benzinger saw him, walking in his direction past the Volunteer Firemen Memorial. He was dressed in dark clothes as usual and had a baseball cap pulled low over his eyes. They met and then turned and walked together deeper into the cemetery.

"You've been busy," Benzinger said curtly.

"The opportunities have been presenting themselves," came the reply. The man in the cap had a smooth, boyish face. He could have passed for a teenager except for the flecks of gray hair that were visible sticking out from under his hat.

"Well, Maybe you ought to take a break..."

The man turned to Benzinger and peered at him from under the bill of his hat. He stopped walking, forcing Benzinger to come to a halt also.

"Seriously. What the hell were you thinking?" Benzinger went on. "You're starting to draw attention to yourself."

"What are you worried about?" the man asked him.

"When I gave you that list of names, I didn't think you were going to do all of them. And you've been getting sloppy."

The man smiled slightly and said, "I guess I have been a little over enthusiastic. Don't worry though, I'll still do your thing."

Benzinger flushed. "That was the deal, wasn't it? Now you're running around half cocked and we are both going to wind up in the shit. Meanwhile that asshole is still running around."

The other man took a more serious expression and looked across the cemetery. "Okay, okay, I'm sorry. Don't forget why we started doing this in the first place." He paused and looked back at Benzinger. "I'll stop for a while."

"Well that may not be good enough," Benzinger said.

The man looked perplexed and asked, "What are you talking about?"

"You other night. You left a goddamn witness."

"What was I supposed to do?"

"You moron!" Benzinger raised his voice. "Why would you go after somebody when he wasn't alone?"

The young man gestured for Benzinger to lower his voice and then growled, "He was going to kill her."

Benzinger threw up his hands and shrugged as if to say, "So what?"

"You fucking hypocrite!" the man said. "What if that was your daughter?"

Benzinger shook his head, "She was just some whore!"

The young man looked at Benzinger incredulously. "You don't get it do you? She's somebody's kid, somebody's sister. No one should have to suffer because they've made some bad choices or been dealt a shit hand."

Benzinger knew the man was on some kind of personal mission and went by his own code. He caught his breath and tried to calm himself down. He lowered his voice and said, "Look, I've already caught some rookie cop and some PI snooping around. And I know that the Buffalo PD has been looking up and down Genesee Street for whoever was with the guy you did the other night."

"Have they found her?"

"Not yet, but the way it works down there is eventually every secret gets out. It's a question of offering the right motivation to get somebody to start talking. Once they find her they get a description of you and your face is plastered all over every police station in the area."

The young man frowned and looked at the ground. Benzinger went on, "Did she get a good look at you?"

The man said nothing. Benzinger waited with his palms outstretched. "I guess that means she did," Benzinger said.

The man still was silent. Benzinger went on, "Listen to me. If you want to finish this we have to be careful. We need to talk to this girl."

"Talk? What do you mean talk?" the man asked as he looked up.

"Just that. We need to get to her before the police do and make sure that she keeps her mouth shut."

He shook his head and said,"She wouldn't. I saved her life."

Benzinger shook his head. "Kid," he said, "I appreciate the sentiment and all, but you don't know how these people think. Maybe I'm jaded but I've seen them up close. They'd sell out their own mothers if the price was right."

The man glared at Benzinger, his eyes barely visible in the fading light. They had to leave soon before the entrance gate was locked for the night. "Okay," he said, "we talk to her. Maybe even scare her a little. But she doesn't get hurt."

Chapter 27

Tom would have paid money to be able to sit in on the interview that Nightingale was going to be doing with Seifert. The detective had seemed genuinely upset that Seifert had somehow been involved. Nightingale might be a bit jaded and inflexible but he was still a professional and Tom had to believe he wasn't about to sweep anything under the rug. As it was, Nightingale was done with Tom for now. He had only reluctantly promised that he would call him the next day with a recap of what Seifert had to say for himself.

So with nothing else to do Donovan went home and went to bed. He was still pretty jazzed about his confrontation with Jenny and Seifert so he had a hard time falling asleep and then slept fitfully when he finally did. It only took a moment for the buzzing of his cell phone to wake him up. He looked at the clock on his nightstand. It was 3:30 AM.

"Tom, it's Dan Brennan."

"Dan?" Tom asked hoarsely, "What is it?"

"We've got a little situation here Tom. I think I have Jack's cell phone."

"What?" Tom said swinging his legs off the bed and sitting up.

"Dad and Peter never found it on him. They thought he ditched it. But then tonight the kid cleaning the kitchen heard it and found it under the broiler."

Tom tried to collect his thoughts. His head felt like it was being squeezed in a vice from lack of sleep.

"Tom," Dan said.

"I'm here." He shook his head and tried to focus. "Did you check the caller ID?"

"I did," Dan said. "Whoever's been trying to call him blocked their number. But they've called about six times."

"Shit," Tom said. He thought about the night they had taken Jack and asked, "Do you have the phone with you now?"

"Yeah."

"Check his outgoing calls. What's the last number he dialed on Sunday?"

There was a pause and Tom could hear Dan muttering as he worked the buttons on Jack O'Neill's phone. "I've got it," Dan said and then read Tom the number.

Tom fell silent and thought. This was bad. By now O'Neill's accomplice would know that something had gone wrong. They were running out of time. If Whitey and Pete hadn't gotten anywhere with O'Niell then the shovel and the location of the bodies from Whitey's past were as good as on their way to the State Police.

"Have you told your dad?" Tom asked.

"No," Dan replied, "I can't get through to his cell."

"Okay," Tom said reaching for his jeans. "Wait there for me."

<<<>>>

Tom had considered just telling Dan Brennan to take the phone to the cabin but then quickly changed his mind. Things were getting dicey now and he wanted to see for himself what was going on. He picked up Jack O'Neill's phone at Donovan's and made his way down to Cattaraugus County.

Under the best of circumstances it took a little over an hour to get to the cabin on Bryant Hill Road, Tom had been to the spot several times. But the sky was clouded over and the road was pitch black. He nearly missed a doe that had darted in front of his car as he was scanning the shoulder for the gravel entryway. On his second pass over a section that seemed familiar he found it. His headlights pierced the darkness as he moved up the half mile of heavily wooded driveway. He'd tried Whitey's phone several times on the way there but it was either turned off or still out of a service area. The cabin was located deep in a valley so either explanation was valid.

Tom broke into a sweat despite the chill country air. He didn't like the idea of driving up unannounced to a hunting cabin with two jumpy, probably armed men, but he had no choice. He finally pulled up to the cabin making sure his lights hit it. There wasn't another vehicle in sight and the cabin was dark. When Tom climbed out of the car all he could hear was the night sounds of the woods, crickets, cicadas and what sounded like a hundred other creatures.

The sweat on his back felt cold as he stepped towards the cabin. Still not a sound or sight from inside. He realized that even though his eyes had adjusted to the dark he could still only see the silhouette of the cabin. He turned around to get the mag light out of his glove compartment. Even through the dark, he could tell he was staring into the barrel of a shotgun.

"Jesus Tom," Peter said. "You scared the shit out of me."

Tom reached up slowly and pushed the gun barrel away from his face. "Yeah... sorry."

"Sorry, can't be too careful," Peter said. "I saw the lights coming up the drive and went out the back." He took a small flashlight from his pocket and turned it on. "Let's go inside." Tom, who was still shaking, followed him into the cabin. Peter lit a kerosene lamp and Tom saw that he was dressed head to toe in camouflage.

"Tommy?" Whitey said, emerging bleary eyed from the bedroom. "What the hell?"

"Dan found Jack's cell phone at the bar," Tom explained. "Whoever he's working with has been trying to find him."

Whitey just stared at Tom. Tom went on, "We need to have Jack call them and tell them we want to make a deal..." Tom stopped and looked around the cabin, then at Peter and finally back at Whitey. "Where is he?"

"In the shed," Whitey said nodding towards the side of the cabin.

Tom had a sinking feeling and his suspicion was confirmed by the look on Whitey's face. He glanced at Peter who was looking at the floor.

"Shit Whitey, what happened?"

Whitey had explained that they had worked Jack over pretty good but to his credit he kept his mouth shut. First, he denied everything but when pressed he admitted that he was blackmailing Whitey but swore he had been acting alone. For two days they had him handcuffed to a heavy pine chair in the main room and then that morning, the first time they freed him so he could use the outhouse, he bull rushed Peter and knocked him over. When he saw Jack reaching for the rifle, Whitey panicked and shot him with his pistol. He'd only meant to slow Jack down but in the heat of the moment he had put a bullet into Jack's heart. He died within minutes. He pointed to a spot on the floor near Tom's feet where the blood had been recently scrubbed off.

"Tom, you've got to believe that this isn't the way I wanted it. I know Jack was our only leverage but he was going for the gun . . ." Whitey's voice trailed off.

Tom thought for a moment and then found himself holding O'Neill's phone in his coat pocket. He pulled it out and looked at it. "Shit Whitey we could be screwed here," he said. He opened up the phone and looked at the display of calls made to and from the phone for the last few days. "Unless we keep it between us for now."

It was after five in the morning and the sky over the eastern hills was turning a lighter gray. They talked for a while longer and then decided to try to get some sleep before their next step. Tom was exhausted and slept uncomfortably on the army surplus cot in the front room. He dozed off looking at the spot on the floor where Jack O'Neill had drawn his last breath.

He woke a few ours later to the sound of Peter making coffee in the kitchen. They ate a quick breakfast of apples and energy bars and set out to find a clear cell phone signal. Tom was in the lead with Peter and Whitey following behind in Peter's truck. They were halfway to Ellicottville before Tom got three bars on the phone and pulled over. They were at a deserted produce stand on Route 240 and were standing around the back of Tom's car. He pulled up the last number that O'Neill had dialed Sunday and hit the send button.

It went to voicemail. It was the canned, robotic recording that came with the phone. Tom thought about disconnecting and then decided against it.

"We've got Jack," he said when prompted to leave a message. We want to arrange a trade." He ended the call.

The three men stood silently, looking from one to the other. A few minutes passed and Tom took his own phone out. He'd missed several calls while out in the sticks with the Brennans. He was just about to see who they were from when Jack's phone chirped in his other hand.

"Hello," he answered on the second ring. He glanced at Whitey who looked like he was going to be ill.

"Who is this?" a woman's voice asked angrily.

"Just a friend of your mark's."

He heard breathing and then the woman said, "I told him no cops, no outsiders."

"I know what you told him. Do you want Jack back or not?"

More breathing and then, "Put him on the phone."

"That's not going to happen," Tom said. "Here's how it works from now on. No more threats, no more games. You bring us the shovel and we bring you Jack and ten thousand dollars and you go away."

"Why would you do that?" the woman asked skeptically.

"We took Jack to let you know that we won't just be sitting around while you try to screw us over. The money is a parting gift. Do yourself a favor, take the deal and consider yourself lucky."

The line went quiet and Tom wondered if she had broken the connection. She came back though and said, "I'll call you back."

"Call this number," Tom said before she could hang up. We got rid of the throw away you sent." After a moment he heard a click and the line went dead.

"Well?" Whitey said.

"As far as they know Jack is still alive," Tom replied. "Sooner or later they're going to figure it out. At least we bought ourselves some time."

Chapter 28

Whitey and his son went back to the cabin to finish their 'clean up' and Tom was headed back to the city. When he got onto Route 219 he checked his voicemail. The news wasn't good.

"Mr. Donovan this is Mary from Haven House," Tom recognized the voice of the woman he had left Allison with the other night. "I just wanted to let you know that your friend left late last night but not before stealing some food from the pantry. The food we can replace. She's not the first and she won't be the last person to do it. I called you because I had the impression that you cared about her and she doesn't seem to have a lot of people in her life who do right now. Well..." she hesitated. "Yeah, just thought you might want to know."

He had also missed a call from the Cheektowaga PD, he assumed was from Detective Nightingale but there was no message. He had hoped that Allison would stick around the shelter for a few days and try to come up with a better life plan. That and she was the only witness to have

seen the person who might be behind the assaults.
If Nightingale had gotten anything at all out of
Seifert maybe they wouldn't need Allison. Still
though, he wondered what it was that made her
want to go back to the life that was destroying her
bit by bit.

He called the number for the Cheektowaga
Police and was told that Nightingale had gone for the
day. He managed to find out that he had been at the
station all night. Tom assumed that Seifert had by
that time either spilled or lawyered up.

He reached his apartment before ten AM.
His clothes reeked of wood smoke and dried
perspiration so he peeled them off and took a long
hot shower. He called Haven House to talk to Mary
but was told she wasn't in. He found himself
standing in his dining room looking down at his
phone, Jack's phone and his laptop not knowing
what to do next. He picked up Jack's phone and saw
that the battery was at only ten percent. If the
battery went dead that could be a problem. He was
hoping the woman he had spoken to would call
before it went dead and he had to go out and hunt
down a charger. Next to his laptop was a pile of
unopened mail. He absentmindedly thumbed
through it, mostly junk, a couple of bills and a letter
from Sidney Ableson, Esq., the attorney who had

presided over the reading of Hugh's will. It was probably the paper work for the Chris Craft that he had forgotten all about. He tossed the letter on top of the unpaid bills.

He thought about trying to sleep but ruled that out. He was far too restless and he didn't want to miss either one of the calls he was waiting for. He sat down in his recliner and flipped on one of the twenty-four hour news channels. After about twenty minutes he closed his eyes, thinking it would be just for a moment, and fell asleep.

He woke up to the sound of his phone ringing in the next room. It took him a few seconds to get his bearings, but he managed to get it on the third ring.

"Donovan, it's Ray Nightingale."

"What's up?"

"This is a courtesy call," the detective said. "Since you pointed us in the right direction I thought I'd let you know what's going on."

"What did Seifert say?" Tom asked.

"The little shit denied everything at first. But around the fourth hour he started to crack and he told us he was having a relationship with Jenny Krupp. He was a little hazy about when it started but it looks like it went back to just after he and another officer arrested Mark Krupp for battery."

"Shit," Tom said. "He was the arresting officer?"

"Yep, we told him we were going to pull the other officer in and go over the report, make sure everything matches up. That's when Seifert got antsy and clammed up."

"Damn it," Tom said. "Are you holding him?"

"Can't. We have nothing to charge him with right now."

Tom almost protested but he knew how it worked. Seifert's only crime so far was bad taste in female companions. "So what's next?" he asked.

Tom heard Nightingale stifle a yawn and then say, "Another interview today, with his lawyer present. He's suspended with pay pending the investigation. I've got to tell you, Donovan, I'm starting to have my doubts."

"What do you mean?" Tom asked.

"We looked up the night Mark Krupp was assaulted. Seifert was on duty, but the GPS in his cruiser showed that he was nowhere near the park..."

Tom's synapses were starting to fire. Of course Seifert hadn't been bold or stupid enough to do it himself. The fact that the circumstances surrounding Mark Krupp's beating matched the other assaults meant there might be a connection.

"You might want to look into something before you talk to Seifert again." he said.

"Oh, what's that?" Nightingale said somewhat peevishly.

"Find out if Seifert has any connection to a guy at Central Police Services named Phil Benzinger."

"For Christ's sake Donovan. I've already got a sour stomach from having this shit head making the department look bad, now you want me to go after somebody at CPS? What does CPS have to do with this anyway?"

Tom gave Nightingale a condensed version of the story, including the most recent attack in Buffalo and the existence of a witness. Nightingale was incredulous.

"That's sounds crazy..." he said.

"That's what I thought too," Tom interrupted. "If it's true though, and there is a connection, ask Seifert about it and watch his reaction."

"You know what I think?" Nightingale said. "I think you're full of crap. You got lucky on Seifert and now you want to double down."

"Hey," Tom tried to get a word in.

Jack's phone started buzzing. Tom stared at if while not listening to Nightingale rail on. The detective must have finished speaking his mind because the line suddenly went dead. He picked up Jack's phone.

"Yeah," Tom said.

"Ten o'clock tonight," the woman said. "Bring Jack and the money and do not screw around. No guns, no bullshit."

From the back of his mind came the thought that Tom had heard her voice before, and not just from their conversation this morning.

"I should tell you the same thing," he said.

"This is it!" she hissed. "Tonight we finish this and so help me God if you try anything or I find out that you hurt Jack..."

"Yeah, I got it," Tom replied. The line went dead.

He grabbed his keys and phone and went for the door. He would have to stop by an electronics store and get a charger before heading for the tavern. The fact that Jack was no longer among the living was a huge problem, but nothing could be done about that. They would just have to play the cards they had.

As he got behind the wheel of his car his mind went back to his conversation with Nightingale. The situation with Seifert and Jenny Krupp might drag on for weeks and produce nothing of value. Allison... she was the only link to the man going around crushing people's skulls. If he couldn't save her from herself at least he could get her to cooperate with the cops and help find the man he thought was responsible for Mark Krupp's death.

Chapter 29

She'd called right before 10 o'clock with more vitriol than ever. If she didn't have her conspirator back they would make Whitey's life hell. When she finished her rant she gave them 20 minutes to get to the corner of Chicago and Mackinaw Streets for the exchange. Tom, Peter and Whitey piled into Whitey's Cadillac with Peter alone in the back seat. Dan would follow in his car at a safe distance in case they were being watched.

Tom looked at Whitey; his brow was creased and his skin looked pale. "This is our best play here Whitey," he said.

Whitey turned the ignition and nodded. "I know lad. I just don't want anything to go wrong. It would kill me if something happened to you or one of the boys."

"You're the only one who's going to be in harm's way," Tom said. "Keep your mind on what we talked about." Then Tom turned around and faced Peter. "You better get that on," he said.

Peter frowned and pulled the burlap bag over his head. "So why can't Dan be the sap with the bag on his head?"

"Quiet!" his father barked.

After much deliberation they had come up with a plan that was at best risky and at worst stupid and dangerous. They would put a scare into the kidnappers and, with luck, get the shovel. The fact that they had killed Jack and had Peter posing as him was still the major flaw in the scenario.

They drove west until they got to the south end of Ohio Street and then took Ohio to Chicago. Whitey pulled up to the curb near the corner of Mackinaw.

They were in the heart of the city's old manufacturing district. In the dim light to their left was a large vacant lot, overgrown with weeds that ran all the way to one of the old grain mills. To their right was a boarded up truck terminal. In front of them in the distance loomed the thirty-three-story HSBC center. It was deathly quiet, not even the sounds of the nearby I-190 reached them. Tom had his phone and Jack's phone in his lap. He had an open line with Dan, whom he hoped was staying out of sight. They sat in silence and waited. Whitey had killed the lights and turned off the engine.

After a few minutes that seemed to drag by, in the distance they saw a car make a sharp right off of Miami Street onto Chicago and race towards then. The car got to about twenty yards in front of them when the driver swung onto their side of the road and turned on his high beams.

"Shit," Whitey said, shielding his eyes. Tom was about to tell him to turn the Caddy's lights on when Jack's phone started chirping. "Send Jack out now," the woman demanded when Tom answered.

"Whoa, hold on," Tom said. "Nobody is getting out of this car until you kill the lights." He wasn't concerned about being shot, he knew they wouldn't as long as they thought Jack was alive and well in the back seat with a bag over his head. He wanted to keep the ruse up as long as possible.

"I warned you," the woman started.

Tom pulled his 9 mm out from under his thigh and made a show of pointing it in the direction of Peter's head. He had double and triple checked to ensure that the chamber was empty and the safety was on. Still his stomach churned and he felt lightheaded. After five years he could still see the faces of the men he had killed at the McKinley housing projects. He fought back the bile rising in his throat and handed the phone to Whitey.

Whitey had seen Tom turn green and understood almost immediately. He took the phone and when the woman paused to take a breath from her diatribe he said. "Turn off the lights or he dies." He said it without excitement, rather in an ominous, matter of fact tone.

Nothing for a second and then the other car's lights went out. It took a moment for Tom's eyes to adjust to the weak light of the nearby streetlights. He looked at Whitey who looked grave and determined.

Whitey said, "I'm coming out. We need to talk."

Tom steadied himself as Whitey opened his door and climbed out. He then walked halfway between the two cars and stopped. A moment later the passenger side door on the other car opened and a woman stepped out and then stopped behind the door.

"Turn around," she said. Whitey, who was dressed in a blue work shirt and jeans, raised his arms and did as he was told. All he was carrying was an envelope. The woman, never taking her eyes off Whitey, leaned in and said something to the driver.

Then she stepped around the door and approached Whitey.

"If you're done screwing around bring Jack out." Tom could barely make out what she was saying to Whitey.

Whitey, with his hands still in the air, said, "Here's how we're going to do it. I give you the money, you give me the shovel and then you get Jack."

She shook her head. "You don't make the rules," she added empathically.

"I don't care if I go to jail," Whitey said. "If that's the worst thing that can happen to me. I can't say your friend will be so lucky."

Tom stared hard at the woman, trying to make out her features in the dim light. She was about 5' 10" and had graying hair that she was wearing down. The voice though... he stared harder at her and pictured her with her hair pulled back and he knew.

"Holy shit," he said out loud.

"What is it?" Peter asked wriggling around in the back. The woman glanced at the Cadillac, then walked slowly up to Whitey and took the envelope.

"Just a second," she said. She took a few steps backward and then turned around and walked briskly to the passenger side of the other car. She was in the process of shutting her door when the driver's side door swung open. There was a glint of light as the streetlight reflected off of something metal in the driver's hand.

"They know!" Tom shouted. "Peter, get down. He forced open the passenger side door of the Caddy and took a deep breath. He had to make an effort to breath to calm himself. Whitey's life depended on it. He jacked a round into the chamber and using the door as a shield he raised the Glock and shouted to Whitey, "Whitey, get out of there! He's got a gun."

Tom looked at the driver who was now raising his pistol at Whitey. He swallowed hard and flicked off the safety. He said a quick silent prayer and with his head starting to spin again took aim. The driver looked at him and froze. Whitey had frozen also, standing exposed in no-man's land. Tom exhaled and squeezed the trigger.

A deafening crack and the muzzle flash and the bullet hit the ground ten feet in front of the other car. The driver jumped and then after staring at Tom in disbelief, lost his nerve and jumped back in the car.

"Whitey!" Tom shouted. Whitey finally forced himself to move, turned around and made a mad dash back to the Caddy. Peter had taken off the sack and opened the other door and was pointing a

shotgun at the other car. "Peter! Don't!" Tom
yelled.

The other car's engine roared to life and
after backing into the remnants of a rusty chain link
fence, did a 180, sending gravel and dust
everywhere. The car raced down the street and
turned left down Miami.

Whitey was behind the wheel now looking
shaky at best. "Damn it!" he yelled slamming the
steering wheel with his palms. "Should we go after
them?"

"No," Tom said. He could feel a cold layer of
sweat covering most of his body but his head had
cleared. Jack's phone started ringing. Tom took the
back off of it and removed the battery then tossed it
out the window.

Whitey looked confused. "What are you
doing?" He asked.

"I know who we're dealing with," Tom said
flipping the gun's safety back on.

"What?"

"She's the administrator at the Niagara
County Home. She's the connection between Eddie
Turner and you. And I think the jerk-off with the
gun is one of the security guards there." He shook

his head and said, "No more phone calls, we're going to have a little face to face."

Chapter 30

Whitey was ready to drive to Lockport then and there and tear up the city looking for the woman Tom knew only as 'Peggy.' Tom convinced him to take a day and let him do a little research before going. Whitey didn't understand why at first but then Tom explained what he wanted to do and Whitey finally acquiesced. They drove back to the tavern. Whitey asked Tom if he wanted a drink to steady his nerves.

"Nah, I'm good," Tom said. "Besides I have another stop or two to make tonight."

He wanted to find out more about Peggy and he needed to go online to do it. Maybe even ask Rod Barlow to look into it using his resources. He knew that if Peggy did have anything on Whitey it was too late to stop her now. They just had to beat her to the punch. All of the threats that she had made though, something wasn't adding up.

It was after midnight and Tom was still on an adrenaline high. He stopped short of congratulating himself for not passing out when he had to pull the trigger, but he knew that he had cleared a hurdle. He drove down South Park until it connected with Bailey Avenue.

He found himself cruising past the darkened Sycamore Market. He looked up at the second floor and saw that not a single light was on in any of the apartments. He made a right onto Spruce Street and parked.

Once more, he found the door at the bottom of the stairs unlocked; it probably didn't lock anyway. He crept up the stairs and looked down the deserted hallway. He had hoped that Allison had more sense than to return to her piece of shit boyfriend but he wouldn't be surprised if she had. She didn't seem to have many options and had resigned herself to this world.

He reached the door to Evan's apartment and listened. Not a sound. He put his hand on the knob and when he tried to turn it, the door started to open without any resistance. Without even realizing it he put his right hand on the pistol grip of the Glock and peered into the dark apartment. The latch was broken and that was new since the last time he had been there. He opened the door enough to slip inside and found a switch on the wall.

As soon as the light came on he saw Evan. He was lying on the floor face down with a pool of blood partially coagulated under his head. Tom listened for any sound coming from the other rooms but it was silent. He walked up to Evan for a closer look.

The blood had come from the left side of his head near the ear. His greasy hair was matted down to his scalp but Tom could tell he's been struck hard by a blunt object. This couldn't be a coincidence. The man with the club was looking for Allison too.

He backed out of the apartment, wiping every surface that he had touched with a kitchen towel that he found on a chair. The last thing he wanted was to be a person of interest in the death of a low-life like Evan. Evan's death must have been quick since the cops hadn't been called. Either that or his neighbors were just tired of calling the police. He thought about what Sherry had said about not feeling guilty when a person of questionable character ends up on the losing end of a situation. He felt nothing for the man lying on the squalid apartment floor.

What did the killer want with Allison? Tom wondered. He had let her walk away the night he had done in Carl Greiner, telling her she had to 'save herself.' Had he changed his mind? Tom was already angry that Allison had left the shelter after helping herself to their food. One of the saddest things he had ever realized when he was a cop was that some people couldn't be saved. It didn't mean you stopped trying though.

He cruised up and down Genesee Street looking. All he got were stares and a few looks from the other working girls. He checked a few of the other places where the trade was plied but came up empty. It was a warm night and there were a lot of girls on the stroll but there was no sign of Allison.

At 3:30 Tom was exhausted and about to call it a night. He was taking one last look down Parade Street past MLK Park when he saw the car in front of him slow down and Cherise popped out of the passenger side. Tom waited until the driver left and then pulled up to Cherise as she was making her way down the street. After a few sideways glances in his direction she recognized him and after checking up and down the street, got into the Chevy. She gave Tom a smile but she looked exhausted. Before she looked away Tom saw the black eye that she had tried to conceal with makeup.

He couldn't help himself from asking, "What happened to your eye?"

She pulled the sun visor down looking for a mirror that wasn't there. "Nothing," she said. "Just got into it with this dusty ass bitch on Fillmore."

He let that sink in and then said, "Have you seen Allison?"

She nodded. Obviously she knew that Tom was one of the few people trying to help her friend. "Yesterday," Cherise said. "She was in the park, just sitting there."

"Did you talk to her?"

"Yeah, I asked her what she was doing, you know? If she had someplace to go. I told her she could stay with me and my friend but she said she wanted to get away from here, didn't want to run into Evan."

She won't have to worry about that, Tom thought. Then he said, "Evan's not her problem right now Cherise. The guy who did her John last week is looking for her."

She looked at him skeptically, "What does he want?"

"I don't know, but I don't think it's good."

"I don't understand."

"I know," Tom interrupted. "I just want to warn her. Do you know where she went?"

Cherise dug into her shoulder bag and took out her cell phone. She pulled up the list of dialed calls and started scrolling through it. "I let her use my phone," she said. "She called this number and then she left the park." Cherise closed her eyes to think and then said, "She talked to some guy named Rondo."

Tom pulled over and took out his notebook to write the number down. He looked over at Cherise whose eyes were half closed and makeup smeared. How long did she have? He thought about the scene at Evan's apartment. "Can you take a couple of days off?" he asked.

She looked at him curiously and then said, "I just need a little sleep..."

"That's not what I'm talking about," Tom said. "This person, or persons, looking for Allison isn't shy about hurting people."

"It's sweet of you to worry Thomas."

He was too tired to engage in a back and forth with Cherise. "I'm not kidding. If you have to go out, watch yourself. It may be more than one guy that's involved. Please Cherise."

She must have picked up on how serious he was because she nodded and said, "I could use a little down time. You know, recharge the batteries." She smiled again and started to open her door.

"Can I drop you somewhere?" Tom asked.

She smiled one more time and said, "I'll be fine. I'm right around the corner. Thank you Tom." She shut the door and glided off.

Tom sat there with the motor running looking down at the phone number on the notebook. It was 4:00 AM. Calling was probably out of the question. He wanted to find Allison in the worst possible way but his time was not his own. Whitey was picking him up in a few hours and he had to get home and do a little research. He was starting to feel overwhelmed and realized that one of the pitfalls of self employment was that you were always going to be working alone and would never be able to be in two places at the same time.

Chapter 31

Tom headed for home, but he knew sleep was not an option. He stopped at the all night market around the corner from his apartment and loaded up on energy drinks. When he got home he booted up his laptop and got to work.

After sifting through several Niagara County web sites he finally found a last name for the woman known as Peggy. Her full name was Margaret Reagan. There was also a security supervisor with the same last name. The first name was James, the same as the security guard who had escorted him from the county home as well as the man who had drawn down on Whitey. Could he be Margaret's husband as well as accomplice? For some reason, he struck Tom as being too subservient to the woman to be a sibling.

He opened up his public records search program and found that they were indeed married. There was a marriage license issued in Ohio from 2009. He tried to dig deeper into Margaret's past but oddly enough there was nothing before the marriage license, no maiden name, no court records, nothing to indicate she had even existed before marrying James Reagan. James himself had seemed to lead a pretty nondescript existence. He'd been born and educated in the Cleveland area, served in the Navy and then seemed to drift from job to job for most of his life until he married Margaret. There was a record of his last employer being a nursing home in Shaker Heights, Ohio.

He tried to look into Margaret again but came up empty. It wasn't the first time he hadn't been able to find anything using the program, but usually it meant that someone had purposefully covered his or her tracks. He wondered if Rod Barlow had access to a more sophisticated program. It couldn't hurt to ask. He converted the information he had into a word file and attached it to an email for Barlow.

He had to tie this up today. He needed to find Allison and take her to the cops before the man with the club found her. It was fast approaching 7:30 AM. Whitey would be picking him up soon.

A half hour later they were making their way north to Lockport. A light rain was falling as they exited I-290 onto northbound I-990. Tom noticed that Whitey looking anxious. "No need to rush," Tom said. "We can't do anything until we hear from Dan and Peter."

They found a coffee shop a mile away from the County Home and waited in the parking lot. Whitey found a copy of the Niagara Gazette and thumbed through it without really reading it. Tom took out his phone and started making calls.

The first one was to the number Cherise had given him, the number that Allison had called when she borrowed Cherise's phone. It went straight to voicemail.

"Leave a number and I'll hit ya back," was all the outgoing message said. Tom declined to leave a message.

He did leave a message for Rod Barlow, asking if he had received his e-mail. He asked Barlow to call him back when he could.

The third call was to Detective Nightingale of the Cheektowaga Police. He realized that Nightingale was under no obligation to share anything about the Krupp case with a civilian. Curiosity was getting the better of him though, and he desperately wanted to be able to give Caroline the answers and closure she was looking for. He was put on hold for several minutes and was about to hang up when Nightingale picked up.

"We kicked him loose," Nightingale said when Tom asked about Seifert. Tom had expected as much. "That's the bad news," the detective continued. "We brought Jenny Krupp in. What a piece of work that broad is."

"Did she give anything up?" Tom asked.

"It took a while. First the crocodile tears, and then denial, and then she hung the whole thing on Seifert."

"No shit?"

"Yep," Nightingale said. "Said that he was stalking her and she was afraid for her safety."

"She's done this before you know," Tom started.

"Donovan," Nightingale snapped. "We know. Do you think we're just sitting here with our thumbs in our asses?"

"Sorry," Tom said. "So where are you now?"

"We're bringing Seifert and his lawyer back in, see whose story has more holes."

Tom thought for a moment and then asked, "She said Seifert did it?"

"No, she said it was a friend of his."

"Did you look at Benzinger from CPS yet?"

He could hear Nightingale breathing on the line. He'd probably pushed him too far.

"Jesus," Nightingale said. "You don't let up do you?"

"Sorry, I just..." Tom trailed off when he heard Whitey's phone vibrating on the seat between them. He could hear Nightingale saying something about leaving police work to the real police but wasn't really listening. "Okay," Tom said. "I get it." Then he disconnected.

Whitey had answered his phone and was looking out through the windshield. "Okay," Whitey said. "Are you sure?" Tom could hear Dan's muffled voice on the other end explaining something. "Alright," Whitey said. "Send the pictures to that e-mail address Tommy gave you." Dan said something else and Whitey replied, "Good lad. You and your brother can head back now."

Whitey put the phone in his shirt pocket and started the Caddy. "Looks like you were right," he said shaking his head. Peter and Dan had been sent to the grounds of the Stafford School armed with a map and printed satellite photos of the area.

They drove quickly to the county home. The rain had stopped as they made their way to the front entrance.

"So it was all bullshit?" Whitey still seemed unsure.

"It's been a landfill for more than twenty years. If the bodies didn't turn up by now they're buried under a couple tons of trash." Tom looked past the reception desk at the doors to the elevators and corridor. Nothing seemed to be moving.

"And the shovel?" Whitey asked.

"Probably bullshit too. I'm guessing that they got the story from Eddie Turner and figured they could make a quick buck."

"Bastards," Whitey said.

"C'mon," Tom gestured for Whitey to follow him. "Let's start with Turner. They went through the doors, and not encountering anyone in the lobby, rode the elevator up to the second floor. The smell of sickness and human waste covered by disinfectant was stronger than Tom remembered it from his previous visit. The door to Turner's room was open and they went in.

The partition was pulled open and Turner's bed was empty. His roommate, the one legged black man, opened his eyes and a flicker of recognition crossed his face.

"Hey, Magnum PI. You got any smokes?" he asked.

"Sorry," Tom said. "Where's Eddie?"

"He's gone."

"Another room?"

The old man shook his gray head. "No, he permanently gone."

"Dead?" Whitey asked.

The man looked at Whitey, scrutinizing him for a moment. "Last night. Died in his sleep," he said.

"Bullshit..." Whitey started.

Tom put a hand on his friend's arm. "C'mon, let's go downstairs."

As they were leaving the room, the old man called after them, "Ya got a twenty for ol' Reggie?"

They made it all the way to the administrative office before they encountered another soul. A harried looking woman was sitting at a desk listening to someone on the phone. She looked at them with a puzzled expression when they stepped into her line of sight. After a moment she finished the call and hung up the phone. She had a blank look on her face and just stared at them.

Tom took out a business card and handed it to her. "We're looking for Margaret Reagan," he said.

She looked at the card and wrinkled her brow. "So am I," she said.

"What do you mean?" Whitey asked. He was getting anxious.

"She didn't come into work today and she's not answering her phone. That's not like her at all."

Tom thought for a moment and then asked, "How long has she been here?"

The woman looked past him and thought for a moment too. "Nine months or so..."

Just then, a security guard entered from the door behind them. He stopped when he saw Tom and Whitey and then addressed the woman. "His locker's been cleaned out."

"James Reagan." Tom guessed.

The guard gave Tom a 'how did you know' look and nodded slowly.

The room fell silent for a moment and then the woman said, "For Christ's sake, the audit is today."

Tom made an excuse that they were looking for Peggy for an insurance claim and pulled Whitey out of the office. They made their way out to Whitey's car and got in. Whitey was frowning out into the rain soaked parking lot while Tom punched in Rod Barlow's number.

"Thomas," Barlow answered.

"Did you find anything?" Tom asked as he put the phone on speaker.

"Should we discuss my hourly rate first?" Barlow asked. Tom didn't know if Barlow was kidding or not and he didn't have time to figure it out so he just said, "Take it out of my next check."

"Well," Barlow started. "The woman, Margaret Reagan, apparently never existed before last year. There is nothing in cyber space that says she didn't just materialize as Margaret Louise Reagan and take a job at the county home."

"Shit," Tom said.

"Wait," Barlow said. "Now, James Reagan, he's a different story. Apparently he was head of security at a place called the Pinewood Senior Home in Shaker Heights, Ohio until he retired in 2012."

Tom was getting impatient but didn't want to snap at Barlow. He already knew about James Reagan. "Okay" he said.

Fortunately Barlow went on, "Four months prior to that, the Ohio State Police, acting on the tip of a concerned relative, began an investigation into Pinewood. It seems that there was some monkey business going on with benefit and Social Security checks being signed over to one of the administrators."

"Margaret Reagan?" Tom asked.

"Mmm... possibly," Barlow responded. "If she was using the name Maggie O'Neill."

Whitey and Tom looked at each other.

Barlow interrupted their thoughts. "I say possibly because right after the investigation started Maggie O'Neill fell off the face of the planet.

Tom's mind was racing. "Did you find anything else on Maggie O'Neill?" he asked.

"A little bit here and there... divorced, one kid, a son born September '69..."

"Named Jack or John?" Tom asked.

"I thought you didn't know anything about these people," Barlow said.

"Just putting things together."

"Anyway, her maiden name was Lauer, but I went back a little farther and found out she was born right here in Buffalo."

Whitey was getting paler by the second.

"Turns out she was adopted," Barlow read on. "She was born Margaret Dorothy Czerny on December 15, 1954."

Tom was looking at Whitey who was shaking his head in disbelief. Barlow was going on about something on the other end, but Tom turned the phone over in his hand muffling the speaker when Whitey started to speak.

"My own sister," Whitey said. "Jesus Christ, Tom, I killed my nephew."

Chapter 32

They sat silently in Whitey's Caddy. The only sound was the steady cold rain that had resumed, striking out a rhythm on the roof of the car. Whitey was staring at his hands clutched around the steering wheel. Tom finally broke the silence.

"Nephew or not, Jack meant to hurt you," he said.

"I know," Whitey nodded. "But my own sister? What's that about?"

"Well I can tell you from personal experience, you can't pick your family."

That earned him a reproachful look from Whitey. Tom went on, "Besides, it sounds like she's been in trouble before."

Whitey nodded solemnly. "Do you think they killed Eddie Turner?" he asked.

Tom looked out at the rain soaked parking lot and said, "We may never know. He may have been in on it or just a source of information for them." He looked back at Whitey. "What about Jack? How did he get inside?"

Whitey took his hands off the wheel and spread them. "It all seemed innocent enough. He's been coming around for about a year. He kept bugging me to let him pick up a shift or two. Nice enough lad and good with the customers. The till was always right when he worked."

"So how did he make the connection and get his mother involved?"

Whitey shook his head. "I have no idea," he said. "Maybe they were looking for me, maybe Eddie knew more than I thought."

"Do you want me to drive?" Tom asked.

"No, I'm alright," Whitey said, turning the key in the ignition.

Tom took a last look at the County Home and thought about calling the state police or the Niagara County Sheriff but knew that the people at the home would figure it out soon enough on their own. They drove back to Buffalo without saying another word.

Tom was back at his apartment before one. With Margaret Czerny/O'Neill/Reagan neutralized and in the wind he could now focus on finding Allison. He dialed the number of the person she called from Cherise's phone again.

"Who this?" a man answered.

Tom got right to the point. "I'm looking for Allison," he said.

There was a pause and the man said, "Don't know the bitch." And then broke the connection.

Tom had expected a little resistance so he called back and it went to voicemail.

"I know she called this number," Tom said when prompted to leave a message. "If you know where she is there's a couple hundred in it for you."

He plugged his phone in to charge and waited. He had an overpowering urge to call up Detective Nightingale and see if anything had shaken loose on that front. He knew he was on the verge of totally pissing the man off so he decided to wait. After a half hour of staring at his computer screen thinking of his next move his phone started vibrating on the table next to him. It was the call back he'd been waiting for.

"You a cop?" the man asked.

"Nope," Tom replied.

"You her daddy?"

"Not even close."

"Look mother fucker, how'd you get this number?" The man was getting agitated.

"Do you want the two hundred or not?" Tom asked.

There was a pause and then the man said, "If you for real, come down to the Langfield Projects at 10:00 tonight. You know where that is, white boy?"

"Yeah I do. And don't bullshit me. No Allison, no money," Tom said.

"Just be down at Langfield and wait for a call," the man said.

Tom was about to issue another warning when he heard the line go dead.

He'd been down to the Langfield Housing Projects more than a few times when he was a cop. It was less than the ideal place to meet someone. There were few white faces down there, especially after dark, but he wasn't setting the terms.

He was exhausted but knew he wouldn't be able to sleep. He broke down the nine millimeter and gave it a good cleaning, then reassembled and loaded it. He wondered if he should call someone, anyone, and go in with some kind of back up. No, he thought, he didn't want to put anyone else in the jackpot.

He made a pot of coffee and took a mug out onto the front porch. The sky had cleared and the temperature had risen into the sixties. It was going to be a beautiful sunset somewhere. He realized he hadn't heard a sound from the downstairs apartment and wondered where Caroline and

Brandon were. At six o'clock he heated up a microwave dinner and then went back to the porch to wait.

The waiting was always hard. All the times he sat on a surveillance detail or got up before the sun to stage a raid came back to him. That was different though, he'd been amongst his brethren in blue. Once again he asked himself, what was his motivation for getting involved up to his chin in this bullshit? Someday he would have to talk to a shrink and figure it all out.

At 9:30, he put the gun into his belt holster, threw on a jacket and was out the door. He thought about concealing the weapon in a less conspicuous spot but wanted it to be within easy reach if things went sideways.

He parked the Chevy on Langfield Drive on the edge of the projects. He checked his mirrors and the area around him to make sure nothing was moving. There were a few pedestrians and cars on the street but nothing ominous.

At 10:05 his phone went off.

"Where you at?" It was a blocked number on the caller ID and it sounded like a different voice.

"On Langfield," Tom replied. "Where are you?"

"Drive over to Oakmont, 227 and wait. We watchin'."

Tom made his way to Oakmont and found building 227. There was a small four-car lot between 227 and 225. He pulled in between a rusty minivan and a black Ford Explorer with tinted windows and killed his lights. The two buildings were set at an angle towards each other and the road. The streetlight over the small lot had been broken and very little light was coming from the red brick buildings. His phone buzzed again.

"That you in the Chevy?" the man asked.

"Yeah," Tom said.

"Between the buildings," the voice said and broke the connection.

Tom looked straight ahead and sure enough a figure emerged from the shadow between the two buildings and looked at him. He could feel a trickle of sweat roll down his back as he climbed out of his car. He resisted an old urge he felt to pat the gun on his hip for comfort and walked slowly towards the man. Before he could say anything the man turned and walked back between the two buildings. Tom hesitated and then followed. This felt all wrong but there was no turning back.

Behind the apartment buildings there was an access road and beyond that there was a weed-strewn rise up to the Kensington Expressway. The sound of traffic drifted down to where he was. The area was dimly lit with only a few low watt streetlights illuminating the roadway. Tom rounded the corner and turned right, the way the man had gone and came face to face with him. He was a skinny black kid in a dark hoodie, probably in his early twenties. They made eye contact and then the kid took a couple of steps backward.

"You got my money?" a voice came from behind Tom. He slowly turned and saw a second man in a gray hoodie, about the same age and build. He was holding a chrome .22.

Tom tried to stay calm. "Where is Allison?" he asked in a low voice.

"Oh, she's here," the kid with the gun said. "Money first."

Tom knew the kid would probably shoot before he could even pull his weapon. Better to try to reason. "I've got it right here," he said patting his jacket pocket. He waited for a reaction and when the kid just nodded he slowly pulled the cash out of his pocket.

The kid in the black sweatshirt stepped up to Tom's side and was reaching for the cash when Tom pulled it back. The kid with the gun raised it and pointed it at Tom's head.

"Whoa junior," Tom said. "I came in good faith. You've seen the money now let me see Allison."

The kid with the gun smirked, "You got balls, white boy," he said. "Your girl right over there." He gestured to a spot across the roadway. The only thing there was a row of roll away garbage totes. Tom's heart sank. "Mother fucker" he started.

"Hey, what can I say," the gunman said. "She was with my boy, Tiny, and she just stopped breathin'."

Tom's blood was rising. He was playing out the scenario in his mind where he would have to take a round from the kid's .22 before he could pull out his Glock and return fire. He wondered if the kid would be stunned at first and panic, giving him and advantage. Then again he wasn't sure how steady his own hand would be. All and all there didn't seem to be another way out.

"You never said what kind of condition she needed to be in," the kid with the gun said.

Once again the one next to Tom started to reach for the money. Using his peripheral vision he couldn't see a weapon. They were really going to be pissed when they found out that he was only holding thirty dollars. He was focusing on the kid next to him, wondering if he could grab him and use him as a shield when the bullets started flying. He evened out his breathing and got ready.

"Drop it asshole!" A voice came from behind the gunman. The kid with the .22 jumped and turned around. Before he could bring the pistol up he found the barrel of a .357 stuck up under his chin.

"Are you deaf?" the man asked. Tom looked at the man and after a second recognized Phil Benzinger from his photograph. Benzinger had a badge on a lanyard hanging from his neck. The man standing next to Tom must have seen the badge too because he turned on his heels and tore off behind building 227 and into the night.

The man with the .22 finally dropped it and put his hands on his head like he'd done it before. "On your knees," Benzinger growled.

The kid knelt down but when Benzinger reached behind him into his belt he brought out a blackjack instead of handcuffs. The kid never saw what hit him. Tom winced when Benzinger connected the lead filled leather sap with the kid's skull. He went down in a heap.

Tom, seeing an opening had instinctively reached inside his jacket to draw his 9 mm. Benzinger was briefly admiring his handiwork and

Tom started to draw a bead on the former sheriff's deputy.

There was a blur from behind and to his right and his hand exploded in pain. The 9 mm dropped to the ground. He looked at his hand and then up at the smooth faced man next to him. He was holding a sawed off wooden baseball bat. Tom looked at the bat in the dim light. His hand was already throbbing and swollen. There was no way that half of an old wooden bat could have done that much damage without having a load in it. The man with the bat just looked at him impassively and waited.

"Damn Donovan, you are a pain in the ass," Benzinger said regaining Tom's attention. "Although I do appreciate the trail of breadcrumbs you left for us to follow." Benzinger took two steps towards him, he was about fifteen feet away and the gun was pointed at Tom's chest. "What is your fucking problem anyway? A few scumbags get hurt and you and that dyke cop can't mind your own business."

"It got personal," Tom said flatly, trying not to show how much pain he was in.

"How so?"

"The guy you did in Cheektowaga?" Tom said. "He was innocent. His wife and Seifert set him up."

Benzinger frowned and said, "Bullshit."

"Don't believe me. The Cheektowaga cops are holding them as we speak." Tom finished and shot a glace at the man with the bat who was looking at Benzinger expectantly.

"That's what happens when you decide to play judge and jury. That and the collateral damage like Allison." Tom looked hard at the man with the bat as he finished.

"Where is she?" Benzinger's voice brought Tom's attention back.

He couldn't move any of the fingers on his right hand. All he could feel was pain.

"She's dead," Tom said through gritted teeth.

Benzinger raised his eyebrows. "Is that so?" he said.

"What?" The man with the bat said. Tom looked at him and for the first time the man's face seemed to be showing some emotion.

Tom grabbed his right wrist with his left hand and elevated it in an attempt to stop the throbbing. It felt as though the swelling was going to make the skin on his damaged hand split open.

"They killed her," Tom said. He gestured with his chin across the roadway at the garbage totes. "Check the cans."

The man looked at Tom incredulously and then looked at Benzinger and glared at him. Then he turned and started across the roadway towards the totes.

"Jason!" Benzinger yelled. The noise from the expressway seemed to intensify.

Jason didn't stop though. He wildly flung open the lid to the first tote and then the second. When he got to the third he stopped. His face fell and his body went slack.

"Jason," Benzinger said a little more quietly.

Jason looked up at the sky and then turned towards Benzinger.

"What did you think was going to happen?" Benzinger asked.

Jason shook his head. "She had nothing to do with this," he growled. The tone of his voice belied his boyish looks. "She was innocent."

Benzinger scoffed. "Innocent? She was a fucking whore," he said.

Jason's face turned impassive again. He glared at Benzinger and took a step toward him. "Fucking hypocrite," he said.

"Don't," Benzinger said turning the gun towards Jason.

Jason hesitated ever so briefly and then took another step with his hand gripped tightly on the bat. "What are you going to do you coward, shoot me?"

That didn't seem to set well with Benzinger. He trained the gun at Jason and said, "Not another step. You owe me Goddamn it!"

But Jason didn't stop. The .357 roared with a blinding muzzle flash and hit Jason in the chest, dropping him instantly. His face went back to the impassive look and if he wasn't already dead when he hit the ground it wouldn't be too long coming.

Tom's last chance. He dropped to his knees and grabbed the Glock with his left hand. He raised it up as Benzinger remembered he was still there. He'd fired a gun left handed only once, on a bet with another cop at the range to see who could shoot better left-handed. He'd lost the bet. Benzinger was swinging the .357 towards Tom when he squeezed the trigger, aiming for center mass.

The loud report from the nine was followed a split second later by the .357 going off. Tom heard the bullet whiz over his head. When the red in his vision from the flash receded he saw Benzinger doubled over. He had aimed for Benzinger's chest but had missed low and caught him in the abdomen.

Benzinger tried to straighten up and raise his weapon. Tom didn't hesitate. He fired three more times, striking Benzinger once. The ex deputy collapsed to the ground.

Chapter 33

Tom shuddered and rose to his feet. He slowly walked towards Benzinger with his gun at the ready. Benzinger was breathing but appeared to be unconscious. He was laying on his back, bleeding from the wound in his lower abdomen and another one in his chest. Would he live? A small part of Tom didn't care but most of him didn't want another death on his conscience. Besides, with Jason dead somebody had to answer for what the two men had done. The sounds of sirens in the distance was getting nearer, it would only be a few minutes before help arrived.

He never once considered leaving before the police arrived. He was going to tell his side of the story and accept the fallout. The man in the gray hoodie stirred but didn't seem any closer to getting up. Jason was dead, the large hole in his jacket was dark with blood. Tom looked down at his face; his eyes were open and empty.

He walked over to the garbage tote and looked inside. In the streetlight he could see

Allison's naked body, partially wrapped in dirty bedding. Her limbs were bent around her unnaturally and her skin was ashen. He knew he shouldn't touch anything. The crime scene and forensic teams would need a clean crime scene, but in his heart he wanted to take her out of the tote and give her a more dignified resting place. He couldn't take his eyes off her. He'd seen quite a few dead bodies but for some reason he knew this one would stay with him for a long time.

The place was crawling with police a few minutes later. Tom, Benzinger and the kid in the hoodie, whose name was Rondo, were taken to ECMC. Two cops stayed with Tom while he had his hand x-rayed and then set in a cast. Jason had broken three bones in Tom's hand with his loaded bat. There was a holding room at the hospital where he was questioned by two detectives, one from the Bailey Avenue station and a homicide detective from downtown. He held nothing back. It all took about six hours but in the end he signed a statement and was released. His gun, they said, would be kept until further notice.

They took him back to get his car. The crime scene unit was still there. The space between the two buildings was taped off and he could see the crews still moving around, taking pictures and hat there

awking. The

eople was

ects.

e of the

t and

as asleep in

gh to the

e and his

ked up the

lying in bed

e open, he

He was

hen his

e off the

hadn't

rowled

g. Margaret was

n the kitchen

w Connie

erned look on

ne phone

and said, "It's

y nothing, but

, out."

id, "Don't stay

p stairs. When

not he put the

sked once she

ur wife? Does

.?"

ed. "It will make

lost twat of a

prepared for his

. There was a

e line was them

each other

et asked. For

her voice.

g a crack about

getaway

Whitey found his anger rising, yelling something about her son when the light flicked on. He looked up and saw her standing in the doorway with a concerned, her sleep creased face. Whitey put the against his chest to muffle the sound the alarm company darlin'. Probably Danny is on his way down to check it

Connie smiled slightly and said up too late." She turned to go back up Whitey was sure she was out of earshot receiver back to his ear.

"Who was that?" Margaret a had caught her breath. "Was that you she know her husband is a murderer

"She will soon," Whitey repli it easier to understand that that his long sister is a thief and a parasite."

Margaret apparently wasn't vitriol because she was struck silent moment where the only sound on the breathing, like two animals circling ing to resume their fight.

here is my son?" Margar dness had crept into t about makin y in her his anger was also giving way to something else. "He's buried in the woods on the side of a hill."

Another silence followed. He sensed she was about to hang up so he asked her, "Why Maggie?"

"Why what?"

"Why come after me like this?"

"You wouldn't understand," she sniffled.

What was there not to understand Whitey wondered. "How did you find me?" he asked.

"Dumb luck really. Jack moved to Buffalo years ago to work at the Ford plant. He'd seen a picture of Mom and Dad that I had and damned if he said there was a guy at this bar he hung around that wasn't the spitting image of his grandpa. He did a little digging and found out who you were. I know a thing or two about changing identities and it was easy to figure out. The second bit of dumb luck was meeting Eddie Turner. He was really sick when he got to the home, but boy did he like to talk. He said I reminded him of a kid he was at Stafford with."

Whitey was angry, confused and sad all at the same time. For over fifty years he had known he had a sister, somewhere. He had given up thoughts of any kind of a reunion. Now he had one and it was awful.

"Maggie," he said. "It didn't have to be this way."

She snorted and said, "Oh and the newly crowned kingpin of South Buffalo just hands out money to strangers."

"We're family," Whitey protested.

"Family?" she scoffed. "I was six years old when they took us out of that dirty house. The only thing I remember about our parents was that dad was never around and mom cried all the time. What kind of family was that?"

Whitey had no response. Margaret went on, "Well, fuck you Francis. Fuck you for killing my son over a couple of thousand dollars!"

"Maggie," he tried to get in. The line went dead. He flicked off the light and returned to his drink. She was bitter and angry. He tried to remember her as she was as a child but couldn't do it. She had also succeeded in dredging up memories about his parents that he hadn't thought about in a long time. Truly a sad affair.

He had found a family though. First Hugh and his family and then he'd had the great fortune to meet Connie and start his own family. He thought about the paths he and his sister had taken and how things could have turned out so differently.

Chapter 34

July 1969

Sonny Grimaldi was out to make a name for himself. His old man had told him time and again how he would inherit the family business, the grocery store on Rhode Island Avenue, but the thought of waking up before the sun to wait on a bunch of wrinkled old ladies was not to his liking. He was more interested in what his mother's brother, Uncle Sal did. Sal was an under boss with the mob. Even though Sal kept a low profile he had what every man wanted, money, power and respect. For some reason Sal was leery about taking him on though, so Sonny was desperate to prove himself. All he had to do was lean on a couple of Micks and get them to see things his way.

He set out with his friend, Paul Anistase that night. Paul wasn't the brightest bulb, but he worshiped Sonny and would do anything he asked. It didn't hurt that Paul was as big as an ox.

Francis Czerny, now known as Whitey Brennan had done better for himself than he had dreamed possible. During this summer and the previous one, Hugh Donovan had got him a job on the docks of Lake Erie, unloading freight. He ate better than he ever had at the tavern and was a frequent guest at Hugh's home where he had become good friends with Hugh's son Tom, who was a few years younger. The only drawback to dinner at the Donovan's was Hugh's wife, Maureen. She was a good enough cook but her sullen disposition put a damper over almost every meal. Between the work and the improved diet Whitey had packed twenty pounds of muscle onto his already large frame.

After the docks he would return to Donovan's Tavern and help out. He'd even started filling in behind the bar when Marty, the regular bar man, went out on errands for Hugh. Even gruff Marty seemed to be taking a shine to him. Apparently once you got Hugh's stamp of approval you were part of the family.

It was a warm Thursday night and Whitey had just taken the trash out through the back. His back was sore and he was exhausted. He didn't relish having to get up in a few hours and start the process all over again, but he had made up his mind that he would never take an opportunity for granted again. For the first time since he was a kid he felt like he belonged somewhere, that he had a chance.

He took a last drag on his cigarette outside the back door and wiped his brow. He re-entered the kitchen just in time to see a man he'd never seen before exiting the kitchen going back into the bar. Something didn't feel right about it. The bar was closed and nobody was usually willing to incur the wrath of Marty and go where they didn't belong. He quietly walked up to the swinging door that led to the bar and listened.

"Aren't you a little far from home?" he heard Hugh say.

"We're always looking to expand," said a voice Whitey had never heard before. "You know, broaden our horizons."

"So you're taking over all the corner bars now?" Hugh asked.

The stranger laughed and then said, "Yeah right. A corner bar. We know all about you making book here. Oh yeah, and my uncle is still pissed about the stuff you've been pulling down at the union hall."

There was a pause and Whitey peeked out the gap in the door, first making sure he wouldn't cast a shadow. The man he'd seen exiting the kitchen was standing with his back to him, obscuring his view of the rest of the bar. He wasn't the one talking though, there was another man probably closer to the bar, talking to Hugh. The man with his back to him lowered his right hand and Whitey saw the gun.

"Did Sal send you?" Hugh asked.

"Nope, this is gong to be a gift to him from me."

From the kitchen Whitey heard Marty say something that he couldn't make out. Whatever it was, it must not have been pleasant because the man shouted, "Shut the fuck up, you goddamned ape!"

As scared as Whitey was he knew that the man's outburst would draw everyone's attention. He quietly pushed open the door and walked up to the man with his back to him.

Hugh was yelling now, "Alright, Jesus take it easy."

Whitey grabbed the man's wrist with his right hand and wrapped his left arm around the man's throat. The smell of aftershave mixed with perspiration was overpowering but this wasn't a formal dance. The man's powerful shoulders bucked but he couldn't dislodge Whitey's grip. While he was trying to catch his breath Whitey squeezed his gun hand at the base of the fingers until he heard small bones start popping.

Sonny finally swung his attention towards his partner. "What the fuck?"

Anistase seemed to recover a bit, or maybe it was adrenaline. He pushed back hard with his legs and drove Whitey into the wall. Whitey felt something dig into his back but he kept his grip on Anistase's throat.

"Hey!" Sonny yelled. He swung his gun towards the two struggling men and stepped toward them. "Let him go!"

Anistase kept thrashing and the two men fell into the kitchen door and then through it. They crashed into the wooden butcher block and then rolled onto the wet floor with Whitey on top. He thought he might have broken a rib when he hit the table but he never loosened his grip.

Sonny was just about to follow them into the kitchen when Marty, who had quickly come over the bar in a move that belied his size, hit him in the back of the head with the bat. Sonny crashed through the kitchen door in a heap.

Anistase's left arm was pinned underneath him. With his broken right hand he was vainly trying to claw at Whitey's face. As fatigued as Whitey was, his survival instincts told him to keep squeezing. After a few minutes Anistase stopped struggling. Whitey was too scared to let go so he just lay there with his arm still around the dead man's throat.

"Kid. Kid," Hugh's voice came through finally.

Whitey rolled off the body and looked up at Hugh, who was standing over him with a sawed off shotgun. It took a second but a searing pain let him know that something had happened to his back.

"Can you stand up," Hugh asked.

Whitey unsteadily got to his feet. Hugh grabbed him by the arm and turned him to look at this back. "That's a pretty deep cut. Probably need a couple of stitches."

"Mr. Donovan..." Whitey started but couldn't breath well enough to continue.

"Marty!" Hugh yelled. Marty appeared instantly in the kitchen. His face was beet red but otherwise he looked as calm as could be. Hugh looked at him and said, "Call the Kelly brothers and get this mess down to the boatyard." Without a word Marty went back out to the bar. Hugh grabbed a clean towel and turned back to Whitey. "Take your shirt off," he said.

Hugh spread a blanket over the back seat of his Chrysler and loaded Whitey inside for the trip to the ER. The injury could be explained easily enough as a fall on a greasy kitchen floor.

Even at the age of eighteen, Whitey was worldly enough to know that he may have just touched off a shit storm. Sal "The Undertaker" Manzella was no one to be trifled with, and Whitey had just played a major part in the death of Sal's nephew.

"I'm sorry," he said breathlessly from the back seat.

Hugh made eye contact with him in the rearview mirror. "Well, that could have gone differently" he said.

"Mr. Donovan... I..." words failed him.

"Jesus kid, just shut up and try not to bleed all over my back seat." Satisfied that Whitey had stopped he went on. "Look, the situation with Sonny back there was going to be resolved one way or the other. The way I look at it is we just took a shortcut. If I'm right in what I'm thinking his uncle wasn't behind this so he was freelancing and guess what? Tonight he and his goomba buddy are just going to disappear."

"But," Whitey tried again.

They had pulled up in front of the ER at Mercy Hospital and Hugh turned around in his seat to look at him. "Kid, listen to me. What's done is done. Even if Sal does wonder where his nephew went he'll never know for sure. One thing I've learned is that guys are more scared of what they don't know than what they do know." Hugh got out and opened Whitey's door.

"Mr. Donovan," Whitey wheezed. "I gotta be at work in two hours."

Hugh shook his head and laughed. "You stubborn Polack. You're done at the docks. I have a full time job for you. And let's drop the 'Mr. Donovan' okay? Call me Hugh."

Chapter 35

Tom had a serious headache and his hand was throbbing again, but that wasn't what woke him up. Someone was ringing his doorbell. He made his way stiffly through the apartment and when he got to the landing could see his mother through the window in the downstairs door.

"My God Tom, are you alright?" she asked as soon as he opened the door.

"I'm fine Ma. Come on in."

They went to the kitchen and he gave her a sanitized version of his night at the Langfield Homes while she listened with concern in her large brown eyes. He avoided going into detail. She had always been uneasy with his line of work and the danger involved. Tom attributed it mostly to the violent deaths of his father and sister.

When he was finished she said, "Tom, you promised me."

"I know Ma."

Rose looked down at her hands. Tom saw that there was something different about her now.

In the past she would not have sought him out to hear about his misadventures and when they did speak of them she would just withdraw into silence.

"That poor girl," she said.

Tom nodded. He had nothing to add to that.

She sighed and looked up at him and then at the cast on his hand and said, "How bad is it?"

"Well, the orthopedist said I wouldn't need surgery. It should heal alright but there may be a problem with arthritis."

She stood up and walked over to him and put her hand on his cheek. "Well, you're too old for me to tell you what to do but for my sake would you consider a different line of work?"

He smiled at his mother and said, "Yes ma'am."

She stayed for another half hour and they talked over coffee. She seemed a little more at ease as she was leaving. He walked her to her car and then she turned and said, "Oh, I bumped into your downstairs neighbor. She wants to talk to you when you get a chance." She looked at him oddly and said, "She's a lovely girl."

"She is, and nice too," Tom replied holding his mother's door open.

"Is she married?"

Tom smirked at his mother. "I'll call you," he said and closed the door for her.

Tom went and knocked on Caroline's door. She must have left while his mother was there because no one answered. He went upstairs and took his phone off the nightstand; the battery was dead. When he plugged it into the charger he saw that he had missed a dozen calls. Most of the numbers he didn't recognize. Of the three he did, one was from Bob Stanley the lawyer. Stanley had left a message for Tom to call him ASAP.

"I take it you're in need of representation?" Stanley said as soon as he picked up.

"I am Bob but–"

"Never mind that," Stanley interrupted. "What did the cops say?"

"Not to leave town, in so many words."

"And you gave a statement?" the lawyer asked.

"Brief one. They said they'll want more later."

"Good, that will give us time. From now on everything goes through this office, the police, the press, everything. When can you get in here?"

"Bob..." Tom felt like he was being steam rolled.

"What?"

"It's just that," Tom hesitated. Stanley was a good lawyer, so good that he wasn't cheap.

Stanley seemed to read his mind. "Don't worry about my bill. You can work it off," he said.

"That's a lot of work," Tom said sheepishly.

Stanley laughed, which was unusual. "Don't worry," he said, "we'll work out something where you won't starve to death."

Stanley briefed Tom on what he had picked up from the news outlets and a source he had inside the Buffalo PD. Benzinger had survived and was in critical condition. He had been hit in the upper chest, narrowly missing an artery, and in the lower abdomen, piercing his liver. He was being held under guard at ECMC as a person of interest in a multi jurisdictional investigation. Tom wondered if that meant that the Krupp case had broken and come back on Benzinger.

Tom cringed and his heart sank when Stanley told him that the police weren't releasing Allison's name because they couldn't locate her family. How far off the grid had she fallen? Even in death there was no one around to take care of her.

Rondo Watts was being held in her death. So far he hadn't given up anything on his friend "Tiny" but Tom doubted he would take the heat all on his own.

The loaded bat recovered was a hot piece of property apparently. It was being scrutinized, measured and photographed and had the attention of a number of agencies that now considered that it might be the key to several of their open cases. The man who had been wielding the bat's full name was Jason R. Quigley, aged twenty-seven at the time of his death. He'd never been in trouble with the law before. He was unmarried and had no family. Police didn't seem to know much about him at this point, only that he was a licensed family crisis counselor.

Chapter 36

Nine months before.

Jason Quigley sat in his office staring down at his notes without really reading them. Maybe he was in the wrong line of work. Kelsey Benzinger was damaged goods, addicted to heroine and abused and sexually assaulted by her piece of crap boyfriend.

Her father wasn't much better off. He was angry and his anger had already cost him his job as a Sheriff's Deputy. Now Jason had another meeting with him.

It didn't take long for Benzinger's anger to flare up. He was seething within minutes.

"Kelsey was never an angel, I know that," he said, "but this asshole took everything from her!"

Jason was trying to speak as calmly as possible and still get a word in. "Mr. Benzinger, we really need to focus on what we can do for her moving forward."

"Moving forward?" Benzinger snapped. "I know my daughter. I can see it in her eyes. There's no coming back from where she is."

Jason was getting frustrated. "I admit it may take a while and it's not going to be easy."

Benzinger stood up and pointed across the desk at Jason. "You fucking people are all the same," he yelled. "All you do is talk and talk about stuff you read out of a textbook!"

Something in Jason flared up now and he fought the urge to jump up and break Benzinger's finger off. He took a breath and said, "Getting angry is not going to help."

Benzinger swiped his hand across Jason's desk sending a stack of files flying. "You don't get it do you?" he yelled. "We can sit here and hold hands 'til the end of time and Kelsey will never be the same and the asshole that did it to her is walking around laughing about it!"

Jason started to see red. Benzinger went on, "What the fuck do you know about it anyway? What have you ever lost?"

Jason had taken counseling courses at UB with his foster parents' blessing. He had hoped that instead of burying the pain and trauma of his childhood he could use the experience and empathy to help others. It would be cathartic. Now here was this man, screaming red faced at him about how he didn't get it. Instead of healing, he felt an old wound, reopened and raw. He stood up and Benzinger, somewhat surprised, shut up.

"I know!" Jason hissed.

"You know what?" Benzinger asked, trying to get his own anger back up.

Jason wouldn't back down though. "You and everybody else who comes through that door think you have some kind of exclusive right to grief and anger. You shoot your mouth off about how unfair life is and what a shitty deal you got."

"What shitty deal did you get?" Benzinger shot back.

Jason's head was swimming. In the two years he had been on the job he had never let anyone push his buttons. He would wonder later if it was Benzinger or just his own simmering frustration that made him take action.

"My mother's boyfriend killed her when I was eleven."

Benzinger backed down slightly. He wasn't ready to give up what he thought was the high ground just yet. "What happened to the boyfriend?" he asked.

"He served five years on a twenty year manslaughter sentence." Jason looked hard at

Benzinger to gauge his reaction. "Yeah that's right. Five years for killing a single mom trying to get by and raise her son! Good behavior and an overcrowded prison and he was out on the street."

Benzinger finally relented and sat down. He looked at Jason differently. Somehow within a few moments the roles had reversed. He shrugged and asked, "What happened to him?"

Jason shook his head and asked, "What?"

"The boyfriend, after he got out?"

Jason flushed. It was like someone had discovered a secret that he had hoped would never be revealed. He weakly tried to change the subject and that was how it started.

Over his next few meetings with Phil Benzinger he would lose more and more of his professional demeanor. None of his other clients ever saw the widening cracks in his very being. Benzinger goaded him and pressed him while railing on about his own daughter. Finally one night Benzinger convinced Jason to meet outside his office for a drink so they could talk about the real problem.

"Call it revenge if you want, but what about the injustice?" Benzinger had asked.

"What do you mean?"

"Your Mom, my little girl, hurt so bad that

they'll never come back to us and the fucks who did it get a slap on the wrist."

"But what would it accomplish?" Jason asked.

"I don't know for sure. But I can tell that there's something you've been carrying around with you for a long time."

Jason thought it was crazy at first—the thought of two grown men reenacting the movie *Strangers on a Train*. But he would lay awake at night and find himself fantasizing about it. It went against everything he had been told by the counselors and social workers while he was growing up and in all of his classes, but even with all of his own therapy and self-examination the idea itself was cathartic. They would help each other to clean the slate.

Jason was out of town at a seminar when Benzinger made his move on Donny Metz, Jason's mother's boyfriend. Donny had served his five years at Gowanda State Prison and been in and out of trouble ever since. After a few weeks of research and surveillance Benzinger wandered into the bar where Donny was holding the pool table, hustling drunks for money and Jack and Cokes.

Benzinger put his quarters on the table and let Donny win a twenty and a round of drinks. The problem with a dirt bag like Donny was they would keep pissing people off until they pissed off the wrong one. He didn't see Benzinger lace his drink with a ground up sleeping pill he had liberated from his daughter.

An hour later when Donny staggered out of the bar, Benzinger followed. He wasn't worried about Donny getting too far in his girlfriend's car because he'd disabled it. Donny was looking under the hood swearing when Benzinger came out and offered him a ride. The next morning they found Donny's body behind a closed laundromat with a dirty needle sticking out of his arm. An apparent overdose was deemed to be a fitting end for a low life like Donny Metz.

The plan for Nick Atkins, the abusive boyfriend, was to wait a few months. Benzinger knew if it looked at all suspicious he would be the first person the police would look at. No, it had to be done carefully and look like either an accident or a random act of violence.

They were pumped up though. After twenty-one years Donny Metz had paid for what he'd done. They were celebrating his passing when Benzinger almost absentmindedly threw out, "Jesus, there are so many more assholes out there."

What started as a joke turned into something much more serious. Benzinger could access an endless list of predators and wife beaters. Jason was willing to help out. If the courts couldn't keep the animals locked up then maybe a few beatings and a hit and run or two could help even things out.

Jason felt like he was two different people; the mild mannered, empathetic counselor by day and the cold-blooded avenger by night. There were times when he thought about turning himself in, he even considered suicide. But there were women and children, like his mother and Benzinger's daughter, being victimized every day.

Mark Krupp's great misfortune was meeting Jennifer. She had just started as a cashier at the home improvement store where he worked when they started dating. She was wild and sexy, two things that Mark didn't have much experience with. Six months later she was pregnant and Mark tried to do the right thing.

They got married right after Alexis was born and things went to shit immediately. Jenny said she couldn't go back to work so Mark took a second job, overnight at a convenience store. There never seemed to be enough money to make the bills and Jenny blamed Mark and his "bull shit-dead end jobs." She still liked to go out though and Mark was sure she was cheating on him. He told himself that he was putting up with it for Alexis' sake.

Her latest boyfriend was a cop she had met at Town Park. Officer Seifert was an easy mark, it didn't take too long before he was believing stories about her asshole husband. Seifert had to retake the firearms safety course at Central Police Services, where he become friendly with the instructor, Phil Benzinger.

Mark Krupp never saw it coming.

Chapter 37

The next few weeks found Tom and his attorney making the rounds, giving statements and affidavits in the various cases against Jason Quigley and Phil Benzinger. His theory about John Seifert, the Cheektowaga cop, giving up Benzinger proved to be correct. Once Seifert realized that Jenny Krupp was going to sell him out he understood that his only recourse was to tell the truth. Bob Stanley told Tom that given the cloud swirling around Benzinger, Tom's shooting might not even make it to a grand jury.

He thought about it a lot. Any one of his shots could have killed Benzinger. Somehow it felt worlds away from the last time he had shot a man. Was it the self-defense aspect? Did Benzinger deserve it? They were questions he couldn't answer now and might not ever be able to.

He had the cast removed and his hand x-rayed. It was healing all right, but it still needed to be recast. The pain had lessened but was still there. At least he wouldn't need surgery.

He was trying to catch up on the things he had been ignoring for the past month. He took the pile of unopened mail into the dining room and sorted through it. He made a pile out of the unpaid bills. With all he had been through recently there hadn't been a lot of cash flowing in his direction. He looked at the cast on his hand and wondered how much work he would be able to chase down with one hand. At the bottom of the pile of mail he found the envelope from Hugh's lawyer, Sid Ableson. He'd forgotten all about it. All it contained was another envelope with his name typed on the front. He awkwardly opened that one. He opened the letter and recognized his grandfather's handwriting, even though Hugh had obviously written it when he was very ill.

'*Before you sell the boat,*' it started.

There was a knock on the door and when Tom crossed the living room and opened it he found Caroline standing there smiling. She looked more rested than she had in the last few weeks.

"I wanted to say thank you," she said.

Tom didn't know how to respond. "You're welcome" didn't seem sufficient.

"Seriously Tom, I mean it. I know it won't change what happened to Mark, but this was killing my dad."

Tom nodded and said, "I'm glad I could help." Then he realized he had forgotten about something; "What about Alexis?"

"Well, that's the good news." Caroline stopped herself. "I mean if you can call it that."

"Oh?"

"Jennifer has lost custody and her family..." she hesitated again. "Her family isn't in a position to take care of her. My dad has applied for custody."

Tom considered that. Lenny Krupp had to be in his sixties. How would he take care of a toddler?

Caroline continued, "I told him it would be easier if Brandon and I moved in with him and he agreed."

"Oh," Tom took a moment to let that sink in. "Um, when is this happening?"

She smiled again, but this time there was a little melancholy behind it. "Next week."

"Did you work something out with your lease?"

She shook her head, still trying to smile. "Well you know how Mr. Spanikos is..."

Tom let out a breath and nodded. "Yeah." He made mental note to have a word with his landlord.

Tom looked at Caroline. She was already dealing with being a single mother of a boy with a learning disability; now she had signed on to raise her late brother's little girl. If anyone deserved a break it was her. He must have been staring at her because she smiled and said, "What?"

Tom looked away and then said, "I was just thinking about how I'm going to have to break in new neighbors."

She laughed at that. "You might want to go easy on the speed bag for a while."

He felt as though he was losing something. He had an urge to throw out a line to hang onto it. "If you're okay with it, I was wondering if Brandon would like to train with me once in a while."

She considered it for a moment and then said, "That is very nice of you Tom. But you've seen how he is with the physical stuff. I guess if you took it slow with him it might work. I know he likes you, a lot." Her blue eyes smiled as she finished.

"He's a good kid."

Another, brief awkward silence and then Caroline said. "Well I've got to get going. I just wanted you to know how much we appreciated what you've done."

"You're welcome," he said.

She stepped forward but instead of a hug she looked up and kissed him on the lips. It was soft and warm and her hair smelled like lilacs. A range of feelings coursed through Tom's body and mind. He suddenly couldn't recall the last time he had been with a woman. She broke it off and stepped back. In only took a few seconds for her face to flush. He realized that she was as confused as he was.

"Let me know when the move is," he said regaining his composure.

She partially turned and was edging towards the door. "You can move furniture with one hand?" she asked.

"You know, small stuff," he said raising the cast.

She was almost out the door. She turned to say one last goodbye and Tom could see her eyes starting to get misty. After she closed the door behind her Tom stood where he was, trying to figure out what had just happened.

He'd never thought of Caroline as anything more than a neighbor and a friend. She was attractive and possibly one of the nicest, most caring people he had ever met, but still. He felt guilty about the part of him that rejected the idea because of her situation, none of which was her fault. He felt even guiltier when he considered the way she bravely and cheerfully went about dealing with what life had dealt her. Besides that, what did he bring to the table? An ex cop with a couple of thousand dollars to his name and a twelve year old car. He knew he had to be careful around her, he didn't want her to be hurt or embarrassed but at the same time even though he was on the brink of forty he felt nowhere near any position to be ready to settle down.

<<<>>>

There was a phone number in Hugh's letter and Tom had called it. An hour later there was a worn looking man in a rusty pickup waiting for him outside of Murphy's Boat Works off of Fuhrmann Boulevard.

"This key is for the gate. This one's for the storage barn," the man said through tobacco stained teeth. He handed Tom the keys and climbed back into his truck.

Tom stood outside the metal building for a moment. The last time he had been inside, he had witnessed his grandfather execute the man who had run his sister down and then heard him do the same to the man who had killed his father. He half expected to see ghosts when he walked in.

Instead the place was deathly quiet. Most of the boats had been taken out and now were probably docked at some marina or puttering around Lake

Erie on this calm, sunny day. The Chris Craft stood alone, forlorn and ignored on one side of the barn. He found the ladder and climbed over the side.

Following the instructions in the letter, he removed the tarnished brass compass from the dash. It felt heavier that it should have. He rolled up the battered mat that covered part of the deck inside the cabin and found the board he was looking for. It was shorter that the other boards, only about two feet long, and the grout, or dirt, or whatever was between it and the other boards was a slightly different color. It looked like it had been moved. He placed the bottom of the compass on the board and the magnet inside it almost pulled it out of his hand. There was a muffled click and then, with a little effort the board came out.

There was a small hollow space behind it, not large enough to hold a case of whiskey, but maybe a gun or something small. His great grandfather had probably added this feature so he wouldn't lose everything if the boat was raided by the coast guard during one of his late night runs. If not a gun, it might have held money, because when Tom reached in he pulled out a brick of bills wrapped in plastic. There was a piece of paper attached to the brick. He set the brick down and replaced the board letting it snap into place. He covered the board back up the mat and then sat down on the deck. When he removed and unfolded the paper he found it was another letter from Hugh. The writing on this one was steadier, as if Hugh had written it before the cancer had weakened his hand.

Tom,

I hope you found this before you got rid of the boat. I know you probably had no interest in the bar, and to tell you the truth I don't know how much life the place has left in it anyway. That's up to Whitey to decide. The house was a wreck, not even worth half of what Ableson will probably get for it. So here it is, your inheritance.

Knowing you I imagine your first impulse will be to burn the money or leave it on the steps of some orphanage. If that's what you want, go ahead with my blessing. It's your money now. If you do decide to keep it, I know you're a smart kid and will figure out how to clean it. If you need help though just ask Whitey or Sid the Shyster. They're old hands at it. I could have written a check but I think I'm running short on time to make that work, and besides I wanted one last 'fuck you' to the IRS and the State of New York.

I know no amount of money can make up for the things that happened Tom. One of my greatest regrets, and believe it or not I have regrets, is that I couldn't have given you and your mom and dad and sister a normal life. I know the things I did made sure of that.

We didn't always get along Tom, but you're a good man. Take care of your mom. I never told her so but she was the best thing that ever happened to your dad.

Love,
Granddad

Tom looked from the letter to the brick of cash. He could see through the plastic that it was banded stacks of hundred dollar bills, more money than he had ever seen in his life. God knows where it came from. He couldn't bring himself to think about the possibilities. Hugh was right; his first reaction was anger. Anger at Hugh for being such a prick when he was alive and now what was this? Was he trying to buy his forgiveness?

He hefted the package in his left hand, weighing it. He couldn't even fathom a guess as to how much was there. What was he going to do with it? He'd have to think about it long and hard.

Although, he might be needing to buy an engagement present for his mother and Tony soon. Maybe help Caroline with her lease situation, anonymously of course. And he had bills to pay. He burst out laughing while a single tear rolled down his cheek.

"Fucking Hugh," he said.

Acknowledgements

Once again the cover illustration was designed by talented local artist Valerie Eddy. To see more of her work, visit diversifyadvertise.com.

Thanks to Cynthia Lehman for editing and proof reading. Your understanding and insight were invaluable.

Thanks to Mark Pogodzinski and the people at No Frills Buffalo. Without your help, guidance and patience myself and other writers wouldn't have an outlet for our work.

To all of my friends who read and commented on the first two Donovan books, your encouragement and support are invaluable.

Finally, to my family, without whom none of this would matter.